A Candlelight Ecstasy Romance®

"I CAN STRIKE YOU OUT, MR. BASEBALL SUPERSTAR," MARTY TOLD RICK DEFIANTLY.

"Don't be ridiculous," he answered, his scorn obvious in his every word.

She blushed, but desperation forced her to continue. "No matter what you believe, it's true. And if I do strike you out, will you give me the ten thousand dollars I need?"

"Perhaps," he answered languidly, staring at her lithe, slender body. "But only if the wager is worth my while. If I win, what do I get?"

"Anything you want. Just name it."

Silence filled the room, and Marty's foolish offer echoed in her ears. Crimson stained her cheeks as he continued to stare at her. She felt as if she were wearing nothing at all.

"It's a deal," he said in a deep, sensuous voice.

CANDLELIGHT ECSTASY ROMANCES®

FEVER PITCH

Pamela Toth

A CANDLELIGHT ECSTASY ROMANCE®

Published by
Dell Publishing Co., Inc.
1 Dag Hammarskjold Plaza
New York, New York 10017

ISBN: 0-440-12505-7

Printed in the United States of America

July 1986

10 9 8 7 6 5 4 3 2 1

WFH

*This book is dedicated
with great love to my own Mr. T.—lover,
friend, supporter, proofreader, research
partner, husband.*

To Our Readers:

We have been delighted with your enthusiastic response to Candlelight Ecstasy Romances®, and we thank you for the interest you have shown in this exciting series.

In the upcoming months we will continue to present the distinctive sensuous love stories you have come to expect only from Ecstasy. We look forward to bringing you many more books from your favorite authors and also the very finest work from new authors of contemporary romantic fiction.

As always, we are striving to present the unique, absorbing love stories that you enjoy most—books that are more than ordinary romance. Your suggestions and comments are always welcome. Please write to us at the address below.

Sincerely,

The Editors
Candlelight Romances
1 Dag Hammarskjold Plaza
New York, New York 10017

CHAPTER ONE

Marty Gibson leaned forward, gray eyes squinting into the bright sun, and felt more alone than she ever had in her life. Calloused fingers sought the raised seams of the softball she gripped behind her as she waited for her catcher's signal. With a barely perceptible nod she wound up and released the ball. The batter stood firm and the umpire shook his head.

"Ball three."

Groans and cheers came from the crowd in the bleachers.

Raising a deeply tanned arm, Marty wiped the perspiration from her forehead. It was the bottom of the seventh inning, full count, with two runners on and two out. One more pitch and the Bower of Flowers team could be the new regional women's fast pitch champs, or they could be in a lot of trouble. Catching the softball in her mitt, Marty turned her back to home plate, blond ponytail bobbing, and touched her fingers to the resin bag that lay in the dirt at her feet. She took a deep breath as another trickle of moisture rolled down the side of her neck.

Turning, she glanced at the runners poised on first and third. Feet positioned on the rubber, she finally leaned forward, concentration riveted on the catcher.

This pitch felt good, from windup to release. Marty grinned with satisfaction when the batter swung, too high and too late.

Her slim body sagged with relief as the cheers from her dugout and from the small knot of Allentown fans drowned out the umpire's final call. Pandemonium erupted in the stands as the other members of Bower of Flowers charged toward the pitcher's mound, throwing mitts and navy blue caps high into the air. They'd won the Regionals.

Marty was first in line as the players from both teams shook hands. "Good game, good game, good game," echoed down the line.

"Good luck at the Nationals," someone called out as the other team walked away, and Marty inhaled deeply.

Nationals. Arena for the champs from every region of the country. The right her team had earned by beating the best from five neighboring states. Culmination of the hottest season that Marty and the rest of the women on her team had ever had. A good time to quit, her father insisted.

Was he right? Was it time to move on, to put aside the sport she had loved all her life? He called it her hobby, but softball was an activity that had given her many happy hours, including some moments of intense personal satisfaction. Marty knew that her devotion to the game was more than most people, her father included, could comprehend. A gymnast's commitment was acceptable, an ice skater's training schedule understood. Women's softball, not yet. Maybe someday it would earn

10

respect, but that day was probably far in the future.

Marty wasn't the best woman pitcher in softball, but at twenty-five she was the acknowledged best in Pennsylvania. If she did well at the Nationals in Seattle, then who knows?

Someone bumped her and Marty was yanked back to the present postgame bedlam.

"Way to go, kiddo," said the team sponsor, Vera Flowers. What better name for someone who owned several floral shops in eastern Pennsylvania? But when Vera gave Marty a congratulatory squeeze, Marty could feel the tension in the older woman. That and her evasive look were puzzling.

Usually Vera was as enthusiastic as any team member, attending as many games as she could, offering much more than just the financial support of a team sponsor. Many businesses merely wrote checks for uniforms, equipment, and entry fees, deducting it as advertising. Vera was different.

"What's wrong?" Marty asked.

Vera shook her head. "We'll talk later," she said, not meeting Marty's troubled gaze.

Pauline, the catcher, interrupted. "Hey, Vera. You coming to Seattle?" She didn't wait for an answer, but grabbed another player and waltzed her around in a circle.

Marty repeated Pauline's question to Vera, who looked dismayed but only reiterated, "We'll talk later." They were walking toward a knot of excited players in flashy blue uniforms.

"Come on out to the van," Vera called to them. "I've got cold soda in the cooler." The group of young women followed, the volume of their happy chatter rising as they replayed the last game and

11

bragged to each other about how they were going to go all the way by winning the Nationals.

"We'll show Seattle how it's done," the stocky catcher shouted. Several voices rose in agreement.

For a moment sentiment threatened to overcome Marty as she realized how much she'd miss the others if she did quit. Some of them had been there since Marty had joined the team four years before, and they were like family.

Arriving at Vera's purple van, she deliberately put sad thoughts aside and smiled at the happy faces. The women looked sharp in the light and dark blue uniforms adorned with white lettering. They played sharp too, proving over and over that they were a team to be taken seriously.

Drinking the soda Vera handed her, Marty spotted her father walking across the grass. He didn't attend many of her games. She waved to him, feeling the same mixture of pride and anxiety she always did at the sight of the tall man with the rigid posture and close-cut iron-gray hair.

"Hi," she greeted him as he stopped in front of her.

"Good game, Martha," he said in his measured way. "Only . . ."

Marty's lips pressed together. She was powerless as usual to stem her disappointment that his praise was qualified.

"You certainly left it till the last minute," he finished.

"Yes, sir."

He nodded, no doubt pleased with her ready agreement. Sometimes she argued, but today she wasn't up to it. With a sigh and a wide, fixed smile she took his arm. "Have a soda and say hi to Vera," she coaxed.

12

"Soda's not good for you, Martha. All that sugar—"

She nodded. "Yes, Dad. Just say hello then." She pulled at his arm.

The older woman spotted them and walked over, carrying an extra pop can dripping with condensation.

"Care for a cold one, Gordon? This is sugar and caffeine free."

Marty saw the way her father stiffened at Vera's casual greeting, and she smothered a small grin. Vera didn't stand on ceremony.

"Hello, Mrs. Flowers," he said in his deliberate way. "No, thank you," he declined as she extended the can.

Marty noticed the pink in Vera's cheeks and studied her closely as the two gray-haired people faced each other warily. Vera was well aware of how Gordon Gibson felt about women's softball and he knew what Vera thought of him. She'd told him once, in her outspoken way, that he was a stuffed shirt. Marty wasn't sure just why, but Vera's blunt words had hurt him.

Conversation was strained, and after a few moments Vera excused herself and turned away. There was tension in the air and Marty wondered, not for the first time, if it was only animosity that fueled it. Her father was still a handsome man. . . .

With a shake of her head she dismissed the possibility. They were as different as two people could be. Vera, a widow, was independent and outspoken. Mr. Gibson was the perfect example of a middle-aged male chauvinist, a widower for years and set in his ways.

Marty turned back to him. She hated to ask the next question, but it was necessary.

"Dad?" Realizing that her hands were balled into fists deep in the pockets of her warm-up jacket, she uncurled her fingers as his somber gaze met hers.

"Yes, Martha?" She sighed at his continued use of her full name, not objecting only because it had been her mother's. She knew how much he still missed his wife, even though she had died when Marty was only twelve.

"I'll need some more time off, you know."

He frowned. "There are a lot of jobs coming up. It's still our busy season." He sighed. "When will you need the time?"

"The tournament's in three weeks. I'll have to have ten days."

"Ten?" His grizzled eyebrows rose.

"We're planning to win," she said, lifting her chin a fraction. "I'll need the full time." She wasn't planning on being knocked out early.

He stroked his square jaw. "I suppose we can work out something," he said heavily. "I'll be glad when you've put this behind you, Martha. No young man wants—"

He had started on the familiar lecture when a cry of dismay cut off his words. They both looked over to the other players standing with Vera, then Marty excused herself and walked quickly toward the group.

"How long have you known?" Pauline demanded. She and Vera were nose to nose, and Vera's expression was defiant.

The group parted for Marty, their natural leader as well as their pitcher. She stopped between Vera

14

and Pauline. Vera's face had flushed an unbecoming shade of red and Pauline's wore a scowl.

"What's going on?" Marty asked, anxiety knotting the muscles of her stomach.

Vera's gaze dropped, then met Marty's with a mixture of sadness and stubborn pride. "I wanted to wait and not spoil your celebration, but you know how Pauline can be." She ran a freckled hand through her short gray curls.

"The thing is," she continued, "I've sold the shops. I had a good offer and I took it. Only there won't be any expense money for Seattle. The deal's closing Monday and I can't write it off anymore." There were deep lines of concern on her face. "I figured your season would be done after the Regionals," she explained. "My accountant told me there's no way I can get any more expense money from the business without jeopardizing the closing. I'm really sorry."

When Marty walked into Pauline's living room back in Allentown the next evening, the rest of the team was already assembled. The excitement of the day before had abated only slightly, mixed now with the determination of fifteen women working to attain a single goal.

"We're here to figure out the fastest way to raise eight thousand dollars for our air fare to Seattle," Marty began without preamble. A collective groan went up.

"The travel agent spent most of the morning on it, and that's the best price she could get us. You'll all be responsible for the rest of your expenses, unless we find a rich eccentric who'd like to underwrite the whole trip."

Several of the other women hooted. Vicky, an

15

outfielder with bleached hair and long false eye-lashes, commented dryly, "I've been looking for a guy like that for years."

Laughter followed and Marty's voice rose above it. "We don't have a lot of time," she reminded them. "Let's get some ideas. Practical ideas," she added as several hands shot up.

There were suggestions for a bake sale, a benefit dance, and a car wash. Louise, one of the few married women on the team, waved her hand persistently. Marty nodded to her.

"It's going to cost a lot of money," the thin-faced relief pitcher began slowly. Marty knew that the time Louise devoted to the team was a sore subject with her husband. "Perhaps we'd better wait, try to raise money for next year."

Several of her teammates began to talk at once. Others frowned and shook their heads. Marty called for order, her voice insistent.

"Louise has a right to her suggestion," she said. "However, we all know how difficult the road to Nationals is, and all the things that can happen along the way." She looked around slowly as the others nodded in agreement. "Let's face it, the opportunity may never come to us again."

Marty's gaze met that of Louise. "I know how hard it is for you, and I hope that you can work things out." Marty allowed a smile of encouragement to cross her face. "We need you with us, but one way or another, we're going."

"Amen," Pauline added vehemently.

Laughter lightened the atmosphere as Betty Lane, the team's shy first baseman, raised her hand hesitantly.

Marty nodded, surprised that the dark-haired girl had anything to say. Usually she only made her

16

presence known on the field, covering first with deadly efficiency.

"There's one place we might be able to get the money," she said in a soft voice.

Several people leaned forward. "Where?" they demanded in unison.

"How about Rick Stokes?" Betty asked, cheeks a bright pink. "He played ball, and he could certainly afford to help."

For once everyone in the room was speechless. Then Pauline spoke up.

"Rick Stokes played professional baseball." Her tone was one of dismissal.

"So?" Betty asked. "Who would better understand?"

Marty looked around the room. Smiles were appearing on the attractive faces in front of her. They were all crazy!

"Of course!" Vicky shouted, clapping her hands. "Betty, that's a perfect idea. Rick's an athlete," she continued eagerly. "He'll be glad to do it. He can write it off as advertising and it'll be great publicity for his car dealership."

The others nodded, all speaking at once as excitement spread like a grass fire during a long drought.

Marty leaped to her feet. She tried to talk sense into the others, but they were aflame with determination.

"Okay," she said finally. She knew it was the only way to get back on track. Stokes would turn them down flat and then they could get back to practical ideas. For a moment the memory of how good he'd looked in the sports pages and how strongly she'd reacted to the close-up of his face made her pause.

The other women were silent now, waiting for her to speak.

"Who's going to talk to Mr. Stokes?" she asked them.

They looked around the room. Gradually their faces all turned back to Marty.

"You are!" chorused several in unison.

Before getting out of her car the next morning, Marty nervously fidgeted with the blond hair swirling around her carefully made-up face. A last peek in the tiny mirror pulled from her purse assured her that she'd achieved the image she had in mind. Her wide gray eyes were accented more than usual with smoky crayon, and her lipstick was in vivid contrast to the pink gloss she habitually dashed across her lips.

As she examined the tiny bump on the bridge of her nose with a frown, she decided that she'd done the best she could with what she had. Her nervousness was a surprise, considering that she regularly faced complete strangers with the idea of selling them something they might think they didn't need.

The golden hair that was usually pulled back into a ponytail when she played ball or worked at her regular job was left loose. Soft curls brushed her narrow stand-up collar, providing a suitable frame for the delicately curved oval of her face.

Slim fingers pulled at the waistband of her skirt as the thought of confronting baseball's retired home run king tied the knots in her stomach tighter.

Pretend you're selling him a solar greenhouse, she told herself. He can't be as handsome in real life as that newspaper shot had made him seem.

A glance at her watch told Marty that she had to go in right away or be late for her appointment. With a last swallow past the lump lodged in her throat, she swung narrow feet clad in strappy black sandals out of her burgundy Citation and pulled purse and briefcase after her.

The briefcase had been Vicky's idea. Even though some of the papers it contained were blank, Marty did have team stats and a carefully drawn-up budget showing the projected expenses for the trip to the Northwest.

Not allowing herself more than a quick glance at the gleaming glass-and-brass building that housed a car agency where Cadillacs and Mercedes were sold, she pushed open the heavy glass door. When she stepped inside, her foot sank into deep-pile mushroom-colored carpet. For a moment Marty wondered how the pale expanse was kept so spotless, then she brought her concentration sharply back to the matter at hand.

Crystal chandeliers were spaced across the high arched ceiling, their prisms throwing rainbow lights over the pale walls of the opulent showroom. Clearly no expense had been spared to create an aura of subdued but distinctive wealth. Even the receptionist looked like the best money could buy, Marty thought tartly.

The woman was a stunning redhead, wearing a black sheath and an elegant coiffure. She glanced up as Marty approached, a cool smile barely disturbing her peach-tinted mouth.

"May I help you?" Her voice was well modulated and familiar from Marty's earlier phone call. The redhead had been determined to ferret out the nature of Marty's business, and Marty had been equally determined to reveal as little as pos-

19

sible over the phone. Marty had only partially succeeded.

When she gave her name, the receptionist's green eyes narrowed. "Oh, yes. The mystery caller with the athletic charity."

"You could say that." Marty shifted her weight from one foot to the other, getting more nervous by the minute.

The receptionist picked up an elegant cream-and-brass telephone and spoke softly into the curved mouthpiece. She turned back to Marty.

"Mr. Stokes will see you right away." When she rose to point a well-manicured finger toward the back of the huge room, Marty noticed that her figure, though excellent, was a trifle bosomy for the high fashion image the woman seemed to be attempting. Just the type a woman-chasing bachelor was likely to prefer!

"Top of the spiral staircase. Mr. Stokes said to walk right in."

Marty remembered to thank her before turning on one slim high heel, taking a deep breath, and squaring her shoulders. An urge to wipe perspiration from her brow was suppressed as she reminded herself that this confrontation would take a wholly different kind of talent.

As she climbed the carpeted steps, she tried to remember the carefully rehearsed argument she'd prepared. Not one word would penetrate the wool that had suddenly clogged her brain. What on God's green earth was she doing here? How had she allowed the others to bully her into asking a major sports star like Rick (The Rocket) Stokes for money? She had to be insane.

Her hand gripped the walnut banister and she entertained the idea of turning around and walking out. Glancing down, she saw that the receptionist was watching her progress with interest. Marty forged on.

At the soft knock on the thick rosewood door, Rick Stokes looked up from the sales reports he had been studying. He resented the interruption, but Mavis hadn't been clear about the kind of charity Ms. Gibson represented.

Besides the Big Brothers, one of his main interests, Rick supported several other kids' organizations with financial donations. It was because of his interest in youth athletic programs that he'd agreed to see the woman who waited on the other side of the door. He imagined a middle-aged matron in sensible shoes and support hose, with a clipboard clutched to her ample bosom.

"Come on in," he invited as one tanned hand idly smoothed his dark brown hair. That same hand froze in the act of straightening his Italian silk tie, and his eyes widened as a slender young woman opened the door. Poised there like a nervous doe, she was unlike any fund-raiser he'd ever seen.

They're wising up in their approach, he mused as rigid self-discipline wiped all reaction from his strong features. He stood up, straightening his powerful frame to its full six feet three inches.

Marty paused in the doorway, warily eyeing the man who stood before her. He was taller than she'd thought he would be. Better looking too, though that hardly seemed possible. Wavy dark brown hair, richly tanned skin. Eyes a deep blue not even hinted at in the black-and-white pictures. Handsome was too weak a word for Rick Stokes. Compelling, perhaps. Virile, definitely.

Marty blinked in confusion when she realized

that he was returning her scrutiny with a smile on his full lips. She forced herself to venture farther into his office.

"I'm, uh, Marty Gibson," she said, her voice thin and wavery.

His smile broadened as he circled the desk with masculine grace and extended a tanned hand. It was plain to see that he didn't spend all his time in the office.

Marty noticed his heavy gold watch, white shirt, and superbly tailored suit. She'd never cared for double-breasted jackets on men before, but Rick Stokes wore the style as if it had been designed especially for him.

Realizing that she was staring at his outstretched hand, she quickly placed her own in it and he introduced himself.

"Is it *Miss* Gibson?" he asked as his large hand swallowed hers.

Expecting her fingers to be crushed, Marty was instead fascinated by the warmth and gentleness of the clasp. Slightly dazed by the sharp zap of electricity that shot up her arm, she forgot to answer as she usually did when a business acquaintance got too nosy about her marital status.

"Yes," she murmured docilely, instead of insisting on being called *Ms.* Gibson, thank you very much.

"Good." His voice was deep and rich, with a rough edge to it that indicated he wasn't as totally domesticated as the suit and white shirt led one to believe.

Knowing that her cheeks had bloomed under their tan, Marty settled herself into the leather chair he pulled back for her.

In silence she watched as he walked unhurriedly to his own seat behind the massive antique desk. Grateful for the sheer bulk of the piece that separated them, Marty tried to gird herself for the sales pitch ahead. Her teammates were counting on her!

Instinct told her that prying such a healthy sum of money from the astute businessman who now faced her would take part talent, part guts, and part pure luck. She only prayed it was her lucky day.

Looking as if he was enjoying himself, he leaned back in his chair. "I don't think I've ever met a fund-raiser like you," he said, blue eyes sending a message that Marty was too nervous to decipher. "Perhaps that's why I still have a little money."

She colored at the not-so-subtle compliment. "That's why I'm here," she quipped without thinking. "To get what's left."

As soon as the words were out and she saw the surprise on his face, her gaze dropped to the hands twisting in her lap. When she looked up, he was grinning widely.

Stifling an answering smile, she made a show of placing her briefcase on the gleaming surface of the desk. It was now or never, and she honestly didn't think her composure would be returning at any time in the near future. No point in postponing the disaster. She'd have to muddle through the best she could.

"Who do you represent, Miss Gibson?" he asked, leaning forward when he saw the briefcase. Vicky had been right; it added the perfect touch.

"I appreciate your taking the time to see me," she said evasively, glad to hear that her voice had regained its former strength. She felt her confidence return. After all, he was only a man.

God, yes, he was a man. Every virile, pulsating inch of him, exclaimed an imp within her. Twice as good-looking as the newspaper picture that had thrown her into fantasy land months before. Frowning slightly, Marty opened the case and sifted through the papers, then darted a glance at the subject of her wicked thoughts as he waited for her reply to his question. She noticed the strong, square jaw and the firm mouth before her gaze returned to his eyes. They were very deep blue, set below well-shaped brows and a screen of thick lashes any woman would have been proud to wear. A distinctly unprofessional flutter began somewhere in her middle.

"I've come to ask you a big favor, Mr. Stokes." Her tongue stuck to the roof of her mouth as she spoke his name for the first time.

"Call me Rick." His eyes glowed warmly and his husky voice caressed her like a cool breeze on heated skin. "And I'll call you Marty."

Her pulse did a crazy dance as totally irrelevant images flitted through her benumbed brain. The cover of the open briefcase fell shut with a soft thud, startling them both.

"Rick," she managed to say. The thread of her thoughts had snapped and drifted away on a hazy golden cloud. In a desperate attempt to gain the power of speech, she tore her gaze from his and searched the paneled wall behind him for inspiration.

Several framed pictures of him in the wine-and-white Philadelphia Phantoms uniform hung there. She remembered the nickname some clever sportswriter had tagged him with the year Rick broke Roger Maris's record.

Masterstroke.

24

Oh, what the *hell* was she doing here?

Rick waited patiently for her to continue. Then his warm gaze was edged with puzzlement at her silence. Marty squirmed deeper into the soft leather chair.

"Mr. Stokes," she began again.

"Rick, please."

"Um, Rick," she corrected herself, and once again her voice seemed to back up behind the lump in her throat. This time the cause wasn't nerves but a purely feminine reaction to his smile of approval. His sexy eyes seemed to darken in color as he carefully studied every part of her visible above the barrier of the wide desk.

"Rick," she began again, her voice thinning as desperation took firm hold. This never happened when she sold windows!

"Do you follow women's sports at all?" Oh, bad beginning, she thought distractedly. He'll think I'm some kind of lunatic jock for sure.

A tiny frown appeared between his thick dark brows as he appeared to consider her question with great care.

"Just which sport do you mean? You're not doing a benefit with lady mud wrestlers, are you?" His tone was teasing.

"Oh, no. Not professional sports."

His frown deepened. A new expression of speculation mixed with caution spread over his handsome face as one eyebrow quirked. His voice became definitely wary, as if he were afraid she was trying to sell him a hot car.

"Ms. Gibson, perhaps you'd better just tell me why you're here and who you represent. Some type of youth athletics, isn't it?" The last question managed to convey a hopeful note. He hadn't completely given up on her, in spite of the more formal address.

"Mr. Stokes." She noticed that this time he made no attempt to correct her. So much for Rick and Marty. "I represent the Bower of Flowers women's fast pitch softball team." Not for the first time did Marty heartily wish that Vera had chosen a different name for her shops and, coincidentally, the team.

At least she had Rick's full attention. At her words his chair had clunked forward. He braced his elbows on the leather desk pad.

"The who? Did you say softball?" The last word came out like he'd bitten a lemon. The tone of his voice went from encouraging to incredulous in one great slide.

Tiny tremors that had nothing to do with the blueness of his eyes rippled through Marty. "Perhaps you heard, we won the Northeast Regional Championship. . . ."

He shook his head. He hadn't heard.

"Oh. Well, we did. In Philadelphia, last weekend."

He remained silent, so she pressed on.

"Anyway, now that we've won that, our next stop is the Nationals in Seattle. That's why we need a new sponsor."

"What?" He looked dazed. Perhaps shell-shocked was a better description.

"Seattle. It's on the West Coast, you know."

"I know where Seattle is," he cut in. "My sister lives there. A sponsor?"

"Your sister? How nice."

"What do you mean, sponsor?"

"We need a sponsor and the money to go to Seattle. That's why I'm here."

Rick looked positively mired in confusion as he held up a hand. Marty stopped talking and took a deep breath.

"Believe me when I tell you, I'm tickled as hell for your team. What was the name? Basket of Flowers?"

"Bower," she corrected in a small voice.

"Whatever. Anyway, congratulations and all that. But what does it all have to do with me, and how much money are we talking about?" His stare pinned her and his voice became steadily more remote as he approached the word *money*.

"Well, being a fellow athlete—"

"Fellow athlete?" he echoed, the look on his dark face even more puzzled.

"Uh, yes. I'm the team pitcher, and you—" Marty's hand indicated the pictures behind him with a feminine flutter.

"Yes," he nodded impatiently. "*I* am an athlete, I know that. But you, on the other hand . . . You pitch softball?" He stood and circled the desk, eyeing the slim legs revealed by the skirt of Marty's gray suit. Stopping before her so that she had to crane her neck to look into his face, he said, "I must admit that I'm a bit confused, Marty. I might link the two of us in many pleasant ways." His eyes danced expressively, and Marty's face grew warm at his intimate tone. "But to call us fellow athletes stretches the imagination *too* far."

As the meaning of his words sank in, Marty leaped to her feet, her purse sliding to the floor as she did so. The nearness of his powerful body made her step back until the edge of the antique desk pressed into the curve of her backside.

"Mr. Stokes." Her voice sounded choked and she paused to swallow before going on.

27

"Rick." His voice was laced with amusement.

"Mr. Stokes!" she repeated firmly, finding it difficult to hang on to her temper and knowing that any hope of getting the expense money from him had trickled away with his arrogant statement. He clearly didn't understand.

He sighed and took a step backward. The expression on his face could only be called resigned. "Please continue," he instructed in a bored voice.

His abrupt changes of mood were disconcerting, but at least he'd given her an opportunity.

"And you're starting to repeat yourself." His tone dripped with male superiority. He had no intention of really listening.

Marty had dealt with that attitude more than once during her athletic career, but she'd never gotten used to it. Self-control began to slip away, and she remembered her father's dry comment once when she'd finally blown her top. He'd said she should have been born a redhead; she sure had the temper for one. Fighting for control, she fixed the man before her with a piercing stare. The humor lurking in his face was her final undoing. She cast about for a way to prick his balloon of masculine complacency.

"I'm a pitcher, Mr. Professional Athlete, and a damned good one." She rushed on before she could reconsider her words. "I'm challenging you," she continued, drawing her body up to its full five and a half feet. "We'll see if I'm not in your league."

Rick looked down at the gorgeous young woman who now stood before him with her slender hands braced on her hips and he wondered what had caused her to get so hot. Resisting the urge to chuckle at her bold words, sensing that it would infuriate her even though he wasn't sure what she meant, he asked, "What's the challenge?"

He wasn't prepared for her answer. "I can strike you out," Marty told Rick, realizing the insanity of her words a little too late. He still was a superstar, even though he'd been retired for two years. It didn't look like there'd been much deterioration either. Marty ran a critical eye down Rick's lean body; its well-cared-for shape was emphasized rather than camouflaged by the dark suit. And he'd look even better without it.

She forced herself to continue with her challenge. "When I do strike you out, you'll sponsor the team for the rest of the season and give us ten thousand dollars expense money for the national tournament in Seattle." Spoken out loud, the whole thing sounded outrageous. He'd never go for it.

"And if you lose?" There was a glint in his eye that Marty didn't care to see.

"Lose?" she echoed. The flip side of the deal hadn't occurred to her.

"If I get a base hit off you, what then?" he pressed. The smug expression on his face infuriated her and again she spoke rashly.

"Anything you want. Just name it."

Silence filled the room and Marty's unwise offer echoed in her ears. Crimson stained her cheeks, and the skin across her face became taut with mortification. If she'd only worded it differently. Surely he wouldn't—"

"A deal," he agreed in his deep voice. "But I'll save your generous offer for another time." His grin widened at the stormy cast to Marty's features. "This time"—he emphasized the words carefully—"I'll settle for dinner with you at a place of my choosing." Rick didn't add that the location would most definitely be his own dining room. He had plans for this blond morsel, but he sensed that to push her too far would be a mistake.

Marty considered for a moment. Ten thousand dollars and the team sponsorship against a *dinner?* Maybe she'd been crazy to challenge him, but he didn't have to make it quite so obvious that he didn't think she had a prayer.

She bent to pick up her purse from the floor. "Sounds fine," she said. "I can strike you out without even working up a sweat." As soon as the words left her mouth, she wanted to take them back. Marty was good at what she did, but he hadn't been called "Stroker" Stokes and "Rick the Rocket" for nothing.

"Agreed," he said quickly, putting out his hand. "Three strikes without a base hit."

Marty had no choice but to place her hand in his for the second time that morning.

"Where and when, honey?" he asked.

CHAPTER TWO

Early the next evening when Marty arrived at the ball field, she was dismayed to see that a small crowd had gathered in front of the stands. Not wanting anyone to know about her dare, she'd nevertheless needed a catcher and it was obvious that Pauline hadn't been able to keep her mouth shut. Marty's whole team waited by home plate and there were a couple of dozen other people standing around. They'd had smaller crowds for most of their league games.

Glancing around, Marty didn't see any sign of the man she was determined to best in the contest ahead. His attitude toward women's sports still galled her, although it was a common one. It was a shame that a hunk like Stokes had to be such a jerk, she told herself as she shifted her gear bag and hitched up the waistband of her sweats.

Even though he *was* a jerk, she'd been tempted to dress in something more flattering. Then perversity had taken over and she'd ended up in her baggiest set of workout clothes, instead of the trim shorts and T-shirt she'd first laid out.

Searching the crowd again, she felt her stomach

do a curious little dip as she realized she'd been holding her breath. Perhaps he wouldn't show. At this point her feelings were mixed.

Several people called out greetings as Marty walked toward Pauline and her other teammates. Perhaps it wasn't too late to back out. Surely there was some other way to raise the money.

Common sense told her that it would be almost impossible to get the amount they needed in the time they had left. She'd gotten word just that morning that the entry fee had to be postmarked no later than two weeks from that date.

"Hey, Marty, way to go," Pauline shouted as the team circled their pitcher. At least no one told her to her face that she was crazy, no matter what they might be thinking privately.

"How's the arm?" her center fielder asked.

Marty swung it in a wide circle. "Great," she said in a hearty voice.

"Can you really do it, Mart?" Vicky stared at her intently. "I mean, after all, the guy's a legend." The awe in her voice made Marty wince in disgust.

"He's only a man," she protested.

"Is he as cute as his pictures?" Vicky demanded, grabbing Marty's arm.

Marty smiled, for once letting his image appear before her. "Better," she admitted softly, then tensed with embarrassment at her candid reply. The others were all staring, so she decided to lay it on thick to cover up her slip.

"He's got these very intense blue eyes. Thick, curly dark lashes, wavy chocolate-brown hair you'd kill to run your fingers through."

She really had them going. They were almost drooling.

"He's tall," she continued, indicating a spot

about two feet over her head with an upstretched arm. "And very broad-shouldered."

Vicky's eyes were glazing over.

Forgetting for a moment the ordeal before her, Marty warmed to the subject. "Flat stomach," she added, patting her own abdomen. "Lo-o-ong legs." She dragged out the words, trying to keep the laughter from her voice. The girls were hanging on every word.

Wracking her brain for other titillating details, she smiled and continued. "He's got muscular thighs, like tree trunks, and a tiny little butt." Marty hadn't really noticed his behind, but they didn't have to know that. At her words someone giggled. She was really on a roll.

"Deep voice," she mimicked in a sexy drawl. "Bedroom eyes that burn right through you like he has X-ray vision." She rolled her own eyes for emphasis, noticing for the first time the peculiar expression on Betty's face.

Everything embarrassed Betty. Then Marty saw that Pauline also looked funny, and *nothing* embarrassed Pauline.

"What's the matter?" Marty asked the two of them. "Am I insulting your idol or offending you in some way?"

Betty only shook her head, refusing to take in Marty's annoyed expression. Pauline gestured with her hand.

"He's here," she said flatly.

Oh, God.

Hoping that Pauline meant he was getting out of his car over in the parking lot, Marty felt the hairs on the back of her neck point skyward. Surely he wasn't . . .

She turned slowly, then took an involuntary step

33

backward. "He's here" had been deadly accurate. Rick Stokes stood so close, she should have felt his hot breath.

Her gaze fell away from his face; then she realized that it had settled on an even more interesting part of his anatomy. Cheeks flaming, brain registering that he looked absolutely wonderful in shorts, she forced her gray eyes to meet his dark blue ones.

Was he furious?

To her surprise he seemed amused, a twinkle glinting in his warm eyes and a smug grin pulling at the corners of his sensual mouth. When Marty remembered some of the things she'd said, she felt her burning cheeks advance from rosy to hot pink.

"I, uh, I mean . . ."

His voice cut smoothly across her halting attempt at a greeting.

"Hi, Marty." The full force of his gaze was potent. "This is Don Weeble."

For the first time she noticed the big man who stood slightly behind Rick. He nodded to her, his face bearing the strain of trying hard not to burst into laughter.

"Don's the umpire I told you I'd bring along." Rick turned toward the older man. "This is Marty Gibson. Wasn't I right?"

Don shook Marty's outstretched hand. "I grant you that, Stokes. You certainly were."

She eyed them both with suspicion, but their expressions were innocent. She knew they hadn't been talking about her pitching ability, but there was nothing she could say about Don's remark without sounding like more of an idiot than she already had.

"Are you ready?" she asked Rick shortly.

34

Not answering, he looked beyond her at the members of her team. Pauline and Vicky pushed around Marty.

"Introduce us," Pauline hissed.

Blushing at her breach of manners, Marty proceeded to do so. Watching Rick turn on the charm for the other women made her grind her teeth together. Her teammates fell all over each other like eager puppies. Some team loyalty!

"*Now* are you ready?" Marty's voice sounded pinched and bossy.

"Whenever you are," Rick answered smoothly, eyeing the loose blue sweat suit she wore, with an expression as unrevealing as her baggy shirt.

Even dressed in unattractive warm-up clothes, Marty Gibson was exceptional, Rick observed with mixed feelings. As he looked down into her gray eyes he wondered if he'd been very smart to accept her challenge. Beating her as badly as he planned to would make things a whole lot more difficult between them. One dinner and a warm tumble no longer seemed as if it would be enough. She was a special lady and he didn't want her to be special.

When he'd first walked into the ball park, he'd been surprised to see so many spectators. What was Marty's game, inviting such a large group to see her humiliation. Did she think he'd throw the match to her?

Marty watched his eyes cloud over as he stared at her. Then he turned abruptly to speak to the other man. She took the opportunity to study Rick closely.

He wore gray shorts, tennis shoes, and a faded T-shirt that stretched tightly across his heavily muscled chest. It was obvious to anyone who cared to look that he hadn't allowed himself to get out of shape since his retirement from baseball. Rick's body was like a well-oiled machine, the muscles rippling with subtle power when he moved. Marty's own chest felt tight as she gazed up at his strong profile. For the first time she noticed its predatory mien.

It also penetrated her fuzzy mind that Rick's hands were empty. Despite the large sum at stake, Stokes hadn't done her the courtesy of bringing baseball shoes or batting gloves. The man wasn't taking her challenge seriously at all!

Marty knew that the challenge she'd issued so rashly wasn't a totally impossible one. For years, a famous softball pitcher and his four-man team had toured the country taking on many professional baseball clubs and beating them regularly.

There were several big differences between pitching overhand and underhand that could give the softball pitcher a definite edge. Whether Marty could capitalize on those advantages remained to be seen. Her jaw tightened and her slim hands curled into fists. Rick Stokes was in for a nasty surprise, she vowed silently. She'd set him back on that little butt she'd described so well!

A few minutes later, standing in the hot sun, he was inclined to agree with her. After the little lady in blue had warmed up, they'd taken their places and the spectators had found seats in the stands. There were a few calls of encouragement; then silence settled over the field as Rick swung the bat a few times and dug into the batter's box. He planned to send the fat softball over the trees beyond the outfield fence.

He'd been startled by Marty's concentration and the competent way she had warmed up, not to

36

mention the speed of her pitches and the grace with which she released them. Not bad for a girl.

Her first pitch was a ball, too far outside. Still, Rick's eyes widened as it shot past. He wasn't used to having the pitcher stand only forty-two feet away. Her windup distracted him, and the ball's movement when she released it shocked the hell out of him. The damned thing went up.

No hardball pitcher could make the ball move like that. Rick had heard of two-bit carneys who toured the country playing pro baseball teams, and sometimes beating them, but had always discounted the stories. Now he began to wonder if he'd been hasty. Still, Marty was only a girl.

He breathed in relief when Don called the next one a ball. This might not be as simple as he'd first thought, but he had no doubts about the match's final outcome. Shutting his mind to any visions of the payoff, he stared hard at the pitcher. She had to get three strikes past him, and he hadn't whiffed more than twice in a game in the last five years he'd played. With supreme confidence, he waited for her next pitch.

It looked like a fat one, and he swung. Too late. He realized that he wasn't allowing for the difference in distance and he was way behind her.

"Strike!"

Someone in the stands shouted, "He's asleep!" and several people laughed. Pauline threw the softball back to Marty, and Rick ignored the pitcher's wide grin. Let them think he was toying with her.

Sweat ran into his eyes and a stream of muttered curses fell from his tense mouth as Marty positioned herself, then stepped back and walked in a small circle. The next pitch was inside and almost struck his hands as it hit the bat. It went foul and counted against him. Strike two!

The knowledge that he'd badly underestimated his opponent wasn't comforting. He stepped back into the box, and then the umpire called for time.

"You need a breather," he told Rick as the two of them moved away from the plate. Pauline heard Don's words and her hoot of derision was an unwelcome sound. Rick opened his mouth to say something, then reconsidered and shut it again with a distinct snap. The fans were shouting with excitement, and he liked to think that at least some of them were rooting for him.

Rick watched as Pauline strolled out to the mound in her catcher's gear. Marty stood there swinging her arm in a loose circle, and the curve to her lips was like a red flag to a bull. The rest of her face was shadowed by the bill of her cap. Rick hoped she was baking in her sweat suit.

He felt ten times a fool as he remembered his snap decision to win the bet and seduce her afterwards. Nothing was going according to plan.

Don placed a beefy hand gingerly on Rick's shoulder. "It's almost over, buddy," he said. "Let's finish up."

Rick turned his frustrated face to the other man. "What the hell do you mean by 'almost over,' pal?" he growled. "You sound like you've already written me off."

Don shook his head emphatically. "Naw. I didn't mean any such thing. You're a great hitter, always were. No little girl is going to beat Rick Stokes. Come on now."

Rick muttered another oath as he stalked back to the plate.

When everyone was ready and the watchers

38

had once again quieted down, Don barked, "Play ball."

Rick tensed, holding the bat behind him. Even it was unfamiliar to him. He was used to wood, made to his personal specifications, but it hadn't occurred to him to bring along one of his own weapons. Instead he was using an aluminum bat from the women's equipment bag.

He'd really screwed up all around with his arrogance and stupidity, he told himself as he focused his concentration on the opponent before him. She didn't look quite as delicate as she had a few moments ago, but she was just as pretty. And just as lethal.

She wound up and threw another rise ball. Rick gritted his teeth and forced himself not to swing, guessing that it would break too soon and come in high. His muscles knotted with the effort of not going for the deceptively well-placed pitch. His gamble paid off as Don muttered, "Ball." Full count!

Most of the fans disagreed with the call, letting the umpire know in crystal-clear terms what they thought of his eyesight, intelligence, and judgment. Someone hollered, "New pitcher!" and Rick almost smiled at the absurdity.

Just one more pitch. As soon as Rick took his stance, Marty turned her back once again. She ran her damp fingers over the powdery resin bag and threw it back to the ground. Anything to give her a few seconds.

Should she go with another rise ball? Perhaps a change-up, relying on its different speed to throw him off. What to do? She stood in the hot sun, itching in the blue sweats, wrestling with the dilemma.

When Marty faced the plate again, she was all business, indecision thrust aside. Taking the signal from Pauline, she was glad to see that the catcher's choice was the same as her own. Marty wound up and threw that one last pitch, going with the rise, giving it all she had.

It seemed like the ball floated to the plate in slow motion. Slowly it moved toward the man waiting. Slowly he pulled back his bat as the crowd roared. Time hung suspended as the stick sliced through the air. Ball and bat almost connected.

Almost.

Marty stood frozen, eyes wide. It took a moment for her to interpret the images her eyes had relayed to her brain. The softball hit Pauline's glove with a loud pop as Rick's bat finished cutting through empty air.

"Strike three!" called the umpire. "You're out."

The crowd in the stands, which had grown steadily, erupted as one being in an explosion of noise. People laughed, applauded, and hugged each other with total abandon. Apparently the terms of the wager were well-known. Voices began to chant, "Seattle, Seattle."

Marty's teammates raced to the pitcher's mound, where she still stood rigid with shock, and tried to hike her onto their shoulders. After several failed attempts, they finally managed to raise her and carry her from the field.

During the crazy ride, she looked toward the plate and her eyes met Rick's. He looked as if he'd been pole-axed with a bottle bat. While Marty watched, concerned, he shook his head as if to clear it. Then he turned to the umpire, who wore a silly grin. The girls carrying Marty almost dropped her, and she lost sight of him. With most of the fans crowded around, she fought to keep her balance and a shred of her dignity.

When Don saw Rick looking his way, the grin faded from his face, replaced by a sympathetic expression that didn't quite reach his twinkling eyes.

"Tough luck," Don intoned gravely. "A rather expensive lesson."

"I can afford it," Rick growled.

"I know," Don agreed quickly.

Rick became silent, staring with narrowed eyes at some point beyond the tall trees. Just a few more pitches, he thought, and he would have mastered it.

"Well, I've got to go," Don said, unsnapping his chest protector. "June's waiting supper. She wants you to come by soon. I don't suppose tonight—"

Rick gave him a long look.

"Soon then," Don said.

"Yeah. Thanks for coming," Rick managed to mutter, wishing that Don hadn't been there to see his humiliation.

Watching Marty being carried off the field, standing alone and forgotten temporarily by the spectators, he had a curious feeling of déjà vu. He remembered how fleeting it all was.

"Yer a bum, Stokes," cried the man who had needled him ceaselessly the whole time. "Ya always were and ya always will be."

Rick swung around and stared at his tormentor. The man was dressed in grease-stained khaki work clothes and held a black-plastic lunch box. Rick thought of his own trophies, his plaques and awards, his successful business and investments. He smiled broadly as the other man shifted a fat cigar from one side of his mouth to the other.

41

Then Rick looked over at Marty and his spirits lifted even more. He threw back his head and laughed as his tormentor blinked in surprise. The guy turned and walked away, shaking his head in bewilderment.

Well, Rick decided as he dusted off his hands on his gray shorts, you've got yourself a ball team. Squaring his shoulders under his sweat-darkened shirt, he walked toward the ecstatic members of the team formerly known as Bower of Flowers. That would be the first thing to go, he thought, that dumb name. Stokes Mercedes and Cadillac sounded so much more impressive.

Marty barely heard the wisecracks of the others as they set her down. Her attention was focused totally on the man she had so ignominiously defeated. Instead of the wild elation she had expected, there was the heaviness of regret pressing her down. Even the relief of getting the expense money they needed was tarnished by thoughts of what might have been. She was almost ashamed of profiting at his expense. Rick Stokes was a living legend and she, Marty Gibson, had tainted that legend, she thought dramatically. Tears welled in her silvery eyes as she watched him approach.

As he came closer, she blinked away the sentimental tears and squinted into the fading light. He was smiling!

Mesmerized by his sexy grin, she moved as one in a trance to meet him. The group surrounding her parted, and silence fell as everyone watched the opponents square off. Marty searched Rick's face intently for some sign of anger or embarrassment, of animosity toward herself.

Instead he leaned forward, a strange but compelling light in his navy-blue eyes. "Congratula-

42

tions," he murmured softly, his husky voice making her toes curl inside her cleated shoes. "You blew my socks off."

His words were so drastically different from anything she could have expected that Marty's mouth fell open with shock. She wouldn't have been more surprised if someone had just offered her the chance to pitch in the World Series.

Gazing into the healthy beauty of her face, Rick acted totally on instinct. His arms came around her and he pulled her to him. Before she could protest, his mouth covered hers. Unmindful of the cheers of those around them, he kissed her hard. For an instant his lips blazed on hers and then his arms fell away.

The expression of wonder he saw on her face was deeply gratifying.

"Consider that my consolation prize," he quipped.

Marty realized that he'd neatly turned the tables on her, wiping out her victory with his macho gesture and putting the "little woman" firmly in her place—in some man's arms. She colored deeply as anger ripped through her.

"For the sponsorship and ten thousand dollars, it was worth a kiss," she snapped.

Rick threw back his head and laughed heartily. "You're sure as hell right. That kiss *was* worth ten thousand dollars!"

CHAPTER THREE

Marty walked into the small office of Gibson Enterprises the next morning, and tensed when she saw her father already there.

"What happened to you last night?" she asked, her disappointment at his absence still sharp.

He paused on his way to the coffee urn. "Last night? I had a golf match. Why?"

"Dad!" she exclaimed, exasperated. "I told you I was facing Rick Stokes at Patriots Field. I really thought you'd be there."

A frown deepened the lines in his forehead. "I know you told me, Martha. But I did say that I'd be busy." He poured some coffee into the cup Marty had made him in the Brownies one year, and returned to sit behind the battered metal desk he'd used ever since he'd been in the business.

His calm logic annoyed Marty and she wrestled with her disappointment. Why had she dreamed that he might miss a game with his golf buddies just to see his only child pitch a softball? As she whirled toward the tool room, he spoke again.

"How badly did he beat you?" His words were gentle, his tone resigned.

Quick anger flared at his lack of faith. One hand on the partly opened door, she turned. "He didn't. If you'd been there, you would have seen that." Slamming the flat of her palm against the door, she pushed it open and stalked into the storage room beyond.

As quickly as her anger had bubbled forth, it drained away. Why did she still let his attitude get to her? He wouldn't change no matter what she did. Perhaps someday she'd accept the fact that he'd never be impressed by anything she did and she'd quit hurling herself against the wall of his indifference. Regretting her anger, she began to gather the sandpaper and tools that she and Jerry Bates, her work mate, would need that day.

When she emerged, Mr. Gibson raised his head and pushed aside the papers he'd been working on. "You actually struck him out?" he asked. At Marty's emphatic nod, he smiled. "Well, well," he said, almost to himself. "Imagine that."

"Where's Jerry?" Marty asked him, eyeing the large wall clock.

"He called before you arrived. Said he'd be a few minutes late and for you to wait till he got here to load the truck."

"Huh." Marty snorted with derision. Sometimes Jerry was as bad as her father. Even as she thought of Jerry, a picture of Rick Stokes formed in her head. She wasn't a helpless female! She'd proved that last night, and it looked like she'd have to go on proving it. She stalked back into the office and grabbed the list of materials for the job.

Marty recalled how much convincing she'd had to do before her father let her become involved in the actual physical work of the business. At first she'd assisted him, installing windows and sliding

45

doors. Then she'd seen a new line of solar green-houses at a trade show and persuaded him to look into a dealership. Now they were the statewide distributor for Sunpower Solar Glass Buildings, with Marty doing most of the selling and quite a bit of construction for people who didn't want to assemble the units themselves. She'd taken a course in solar energy at the college and found the whole concept fascinating.

A big plus to the work was getting the time off she needed to play ball. A drawback was the traveling to fairs and trade shows to drum up new customers, and sometimes to assemble kits at the other end of the state.

Lately Mr. Gibson had become impatient with the heavy commitment she'd made to her team, and this season he'd tried his best to talk her into retiring from fast pitch. She'd run into quite a few people who thought nothing of a man's preoccupation with hunting or some team sport but couldn't understand her dedication.

"You don't make any money," they'd say, or, "You can't make a career out of baseball like a man could." She understood that most people thought her a little strange, but she'd been deeply committed to the game ever since she started playing Little League at the age of ten. By the time she reached her teens, she was the first to be taken in the draft each year. After graduation she joined a team of young women who played "just for the fun of it." That was perfectly all right for some, but within three weeks Marty had gained her release and joined a major league team. When they folded she came to Bower of Flowers. She'd never planned to stay in the game until she was twenty-five; it had just happened.

Now she silently agreed with her dad that it was probably time to go on to other things, but the idea was still a painful one. She'd always planned to quit a winner, while she was still in her prime, instead of hanging on until she lost her ability. Winning the Regionals and going to Nationals would certainly be a fitting end to a successful amateur career. Part of her knew that the time was right and part of her wanted to delay the decision for one more season.

She wondered how Rick Stokes had known it was time to stop. That was something she'd never have the chance to ask him.

She checked out the truck, making sure there were measuring tapes, grease pencils, and glass cutters, just in case a pane didn't fit. Then she located the cartons containing the greenhouse wall they were installing to complete a breakfast nook, and waited for Jerry to arrive. She wasn't going to chance dropping a box of windows just to prove a point.

Her father had started the full-time business only a few years before Marty joined the firm. Before that, he'd run a window replacement service out of his garage while working for one of the local steel mills as an accountant. He'd always wanted a business of his own and a son to pass it on to.

Well, Marty reflected sadly, he'd gotten one of his wishes.

As she was standing at the pump, gassing up the truck, firm male hands grabbed her around the waist. Quickly she replaced the nozzle.

"Way to go, superstar!" Jerry's voice in her ear was sweet music after her father's attitude. Marty laughed as Jerry swung her around. Setting her down, he flipped his straight blond hair back from his forehead.

Jerry's passion was body-building and his looks were pure California: blue eyes, light hair, more muscles than anyone would ever need, and a tan that didn't fade in Pennsylvania winters. He was a tireless worker and they got along well.

Jerry liked the job because he could work around the many body-building competitions he entered. Sometimes he came to Marty's games and sometimes she watched him perform. Her friendship with the twenty-two-year-old was solid, close, and completely platonic.

"Nice work last night," Jerry commented as he hefted a large carton into the back of the truck.

"Thank you," she said as he turned to grab another box. "But you left without saying hello."

Jerry slid the crate carefully into the padded rear of the truck. "You could have told me about the challenge yourself," he chided. "I wouldn't have known about it if Pauline hadn't called to tell me."

"I knew she'd be glad of the excuse," Marty retorted. Sometimes men were so dense. She grinned when she saw the color run up Jerry's muscular neck and spill onto his cheeks. She didn't understand how such a handsome young hunk could be so shy. Jerry worked out at Pauline's gym with several other body-builders and power-lifters. She'd been trying to get his attention all summer and Jerry was oblivious to her effort.

Marty placed a hand lightly on his bronzed forearm. "Pauline is pretty nice, you know," she told him. "You could give her a chance."

Not giving him time to reply, she ran to the office and grabbed the clipboard with the paperwork for the job. It was in Williamsport, a drive of over a hundred miles. When they worked in the western part of the state, they sometimes had to stay overnight. But they weren't planning to this time. The wall shouldn't take that much time.

"See you later," she called over her shoulder to her father, who was studying a sales report. If he replied she didn't hear.

She spent most of the ride to Williamsport fending off Jerry's questions about Rick Stokes. Rick had been in her thoughts more than she cared to admit, and having his name pop up every few minutes didn't help in her battle to forget all about him. The questions resumed on the ride home and Marty's patience finally evaporated.

It had been a long and difficult day, starting badly when they dropped and broke one of the larger panes. Then they'd cut a spare piece too short because Marty had marked it wrong. Jerry had to drive into town and buy a matching sheet of glass while Marty worked alone. And they'd stayed two extra hours to get the job done, rather than make the long drive again the next day.

Now Marty snapped at Jerry and hurt filled his eyes before he looked away. She felt awful. He hadn't said a word in recrimination when she'd cut that glass short.

"I'm sorry," she apologized quickly, taking her eyes off the road. "I guess I'm just tired." Her arms ached from reaching and her feet hurt from standing.

"I understand," Jerry said. "Why don't you let me drive the rest of the way?"

Usually they alternated and he'd driven to Williamsport that morning, but Marty nodded gratefully and pulled off the highway. Perhaps if he were occupied with driving, he'd forget about Rick Stokes.

As Jerry started driving, Marty stretched out and rubbed the back of her neck. Wanting nothing more than a long soak in a warm tub, she didn't envy Jerry. He had a competition coming up and she knew he'd head straight for the gym.

Jerry leaned forward to turn up the radio and spent the remainder of the drive humming along softly with the country-and-western songs that drifted from the speakers. Marty was grateful that he'd quit talking about Rick.

Her feelings about the other man were too confusing to discuss with anyone. She had been trying to avoid even thinking about him, with mixed results. She'd never experienced the magnetic pull she felt whenever she was around Rick and she wasn't sure she liked it.

Marty would have liked to discuss Pauline with Jerry, but wasn't sure just how to reopen the subject. Well, she thought with a mental shrug, they were both adults and would have to work out their own problems. She had enough on her plate, with Nationals coming up soon.

When they pulled into the yard of Gibson Glass, the place was deserted. Even Marty's father had left. She went into the back room, stripped off her sweaty overalls and tossed them into the laundry bag. Leaving the paperwork on her desk, she made a mental note to complete it the next day. By the time she got back outside, Jerry had locked the truck and checked the side door of the building.

Marty gave him a weary smile as she climbed into her own car. Ordinarily she would have tried to talk him into sharing a pizza and skipping his

50

workout, but she was too tired. "See you Monday," she said, glad there was nothing to do the next day but paperwork and telephoning. He waved as she backed her car onto the street.

By the time she pulled into her reserved spot back at her apartment house, she had decided that a bath and a can of soup, in that order, would be the ideal finish to her day.

Getting out of her car, she noticed a sleek black Mercedes parked on her left. A low whistle left her lips as she glanced at its pure lines and gleaming paint, so shiny that it looked almost wet. Someone has taste, she thought as she locked her Chevy. The car's owner was probably visiting that expensive-looking brunette in 11-C.

Her weary body tensed when the door of the Mercedes opened, and then she felt a thrill of emotion as she recognized the dark head that emerged. Her heart faltered, then began again in double time.

Rick!

"Hi," he said as he slammed the door. "You're late."

Marty stepped to the walkway. "Late for what?"

Rick's gaze slid down her slender form, clad in worn jeans, snug T-shirt, and shabby Windbreaker with peeling lettering on its front. Her hair was pulled back into a ponytail as usual, but numerous tendrils had escaped and formed a soft halo around her face. The arrangement was free of any artifice and looked beautiful to him. As he stared down at her, the tip of her tongue wet her lip and he felt a tightening in the lower part of his anatomy. The things she did to him without even trying . . .

He would've bet she didn't have a phony cell in

51

her body. His lips curved into a rueful smile. Perhaps he shouldn't bet. The last one had been a disaster.

"I want you to have dinner with me," he said. "I can wait while you change."

His presumption struck sparks off Marty, and his pointed glance at the way she was dressed wasn't a nice addition to a long day. It wasn't the way *she* would have chosen to be garbed for their next meeting either. Her chin jutted in defiance.

"I have other plans," she snapped. "Did you bring the check?"

She wished immediately that she hadn't been so harsh, but the man irritated her with his bossy ways. How did he know she would be free to eat with him? In fact, how did he know where she lived?

She asked him that after he had assured her in a voice edged with annoyance that he did indeed have the money with him.

"I looked it up in the book and hoped that you were M. Gibson," he said. "It wasn't too difficult. Do you always dress like that for work, or weren't you working?"

Marty flushed at the direct question. He was blunt too. "I was working," she said. When she didn't elaborate, he smiled.

"Come on, let's get you cleaned up so we can go eat. I'm starved."

Marty dug in her heels as he moved in the direction of her apartment. "Just a minute," she said to his retreating back. "I said I have plans."

"You only said that to save face." The words floated back on a wave of self-confidence that irked her further.

She followed him, her weary limbs protesting at every step. "Rick," she called, voice plaintive.

He turned abruptly and she collided with his hard chest, only throwing up her hands in the nick of time. He gripped her elbows and held her when she would have backed away.

"Yes, honey?" They were so close that his warm breath caressed her face. Goose bumps popped up along her arms and her knees grew dangerously weak as his tangy cologne penetrated her senses. Her mouth went dry as he continued to look down at her, and her heart thumped loudly. A tremor shook her, and Rick's eyes darkened and narrowed.

As he lowered his head, a car driving by honked and he jerked away, muttering a pungent curse.

Marty became instantly aware of their surroundings and pulled out of his arms. She winced as she stepped on a particularly painful blister, and Rick was instantly concerned.

"Are you all right?" he asked.

"Just tired," Marty answered. "Too tired to go out."

Rick hesitated, sapphire eyes glowing with determination. Then their light dimmed. Marty watched in confusion. One moment she was exasperated, the next her heart was in her throat. It was too much to sort through, and her lids slowly drooped down over her eyes as the two of them stood there.

Without another word, Rick scooped her into his arms. Her mouth was a round O of protest and her eyes opened wide. He liked the feel of her nestled against his chest, but he couldn't press her when she was so obviously exhausted. Tearing his gaze away from her soft mouth, he began to walk.

"Twenty-A, isn't it?"

"Yes," she murmured, too mixed up even to wonder how he knew so much. His clean male scent and potent virility were overwhelming. Marty wished her apartment was a block away, but in only a moment they stood before her door.

Rick lowered her gently to her feet. She looked up at him, but any protest she was inclined to make died in her throat. He was staring at her mouth as a thirsty man at an icy glass of lemonade.

Rick groaned, the sound rumbling deep in his chest as he continued to stare. Marty saw his rib cage expand as he took in a long, slow breath. As she watched, the pupils of his eyes enlarged until the blue was only a thin ring surrounding dark orbs.

She waited expectantly, eagerly, for his kiss, her whole body strung taut with sudden longing. To her surprise, he stepped back and jammed a hand into his jacket pocket, expelling the breath in a whoosh.

Slipping a folded paper into the neckline of her dusty T-shirt, he murmured, "I'll let you off the hook this time. But I should make you buy me dinner sometime soon. With this"—his hand touched the check, brushing her bare skin and making her shiver—"you've about cleaned me out."

"Hah!" Marty exclaimed, the spell broken by his words. "I seriously doubt that."

He ignored her. "When's the team's next practice?"

The abrupt change of subject startled her. "Uh, tomorrow evening at five o'clock. Why?"

"*Why?*" he shot back. "You're spending my

money and wearing my name. I plan to give you girls some pointers so you don't abuse either one."

The next day crawled by slowly as Marty finished with the paperwork that had been piling up on her desk. Her emotions seesawed between eagerness to see Rick again and dread that she would reveal how strongly he affected her. Between gladness that he was showing a personal interest in the team and foreboding that his parting remark of the night before signified an attitude that would prove intolerable to the others as well as to Marty herself.

Had she possessed a crystal ball or second sight, Marty would have been tempted to skip turnout altogether.

A traffic jam on the way to Patriots Field made her almost the last one there. She wanted to prepare the others for Rick before he arrived, but the gleaming Mercedes was already there when Marty turned her Citation into the parking lot.

Rick was searching in the backseat of the Mercedes and a little boy stood to the side. As Marty walked closer, she could see that the child had dark hair like Rick's under the Phantom baseball cap perched on his head.

She stumbled to a halt. She'd never thought to ask Rick if he was married or had a family. The newspaper articles hadn't said, and the way he'd acted the evening before, she'd just assumed he didn't. Her own response to the big athlete's special brand of male charm made her feel like a prize jackass as the boy turned and looked at her.

"Hi, Marty." Rick's voice was open and cheerful as he pulled a color photo from under the backseat. Whipping out a pen, he scrawled a signature across the picture of himself.

"Gee thanks, Mr. Stokes," said the boy in a voice oozing hero worship.

"No problem." Rick patted the youngster's shoulder and the boy turned away.

Marty's cheeks flamed as she realized the conclusion she'd almost jumped to. Sometimes Rick could be genuinely nice, she thought. Every time she slapped a label on him, he slipped out of it. She didn't know how she felt about that yet, or about him, except that one look from his dark blue eyes could turn her knees to putty.

A few minutes into turnout Marty decided that Rick's pluses could never outweigh his minuses. The man was arrogant, tactless, conceited, bossy, egotistical . . . The list was endless.

He'd completely taken over everything, only glancing at their coach, Pat, occasionally. He was like a steamroller and at first they had all been too dazzled by his presence to mind. But now his high-handed attitude was getting to everyone, including Pat, who had gone to sit in the stands. Rick didn't even notice as he assigned positions for some infield and baserunning practice.

The girls were nervous and made mistakes they hadn't made all season. Rick's patience began to wear thin and his voice got louder. Pauline hit a grounder and ran to first, and things got rapidly worse. First, Rick yelled at Pauline.

"Lead off!" he yelled. "You're hugging that base like it was your mother."

Marty walked quickly to Rick, who stood with his hands on slim, denim-covered hips. She'd noticed that this time he had on cleats at least. She also noticed how the well-worn denim of his old jeans clung to him, emphasizing the powerful length of his legs and the bold indication of his sex.

"I need to talk to you," she said quietly, ignoring her own response to him.

He glanced down at her. "Not now," he snapped as he moved around her, leaving the aroma of hot, sweaty male animal in the air.

Marty found herself skipping to keep up with his long strides as he stalked toward Pauline, who stood red-faced at first base.

Marty tugged at his sleeve. "Yes, Rick. Now," she insisted.

He stopped in his tracks and she collided with him.

"Listen," he barked, glaring down at her. "If you girls can't take a little hollering, you've been pampered too long."

He glanced up to the stands where Pat perched, a smug grin on her face. Instinct told him that something was wrong. She should look embarrassed. Instead, she seemed to be enjoying herself.

"All right, you big dope." Marty gave him a taste of his medicine.

He stared back at Marty. What was her problem? He couldn't think why she should be so upset. He knew that women got a little irrational at certain times, but he hadn't expected it of her.

"Well?" He tapped a foot as he waited for her to speak, refusing to allow his gaze to drop to the feminine curves he longed to hold in his hands.

"You can't lead off until the ball leaves the pitcher's hand!" she shouted in frustration. "That's what I've been trying to tell you."

That had never occurred to him. "Sorry, Pauline," he said to the runner. "Positions, girls."

"Hey, Rick, wanna borrow my handbook?" Pat called from the stands.

Several players grinned and Rick flushed. It wouldn't do to lose control, and anyone was entitled to one silly little mistake. It seemed the girls played by slightly different rules.

Marty thought the incident might subdue him, but whatever lesson he had learned faded after ten minutes. Pat had returned to the field and was helping a few players with their batting. Rick stood off to the side. When he made a comment about the infielders playing way too shallow, Pat snapped something back.

By the time Marty had arrived to see what the commotion was about, Pat had threatened to quit and Rick had learned another difference between baseball and fast pitch.

Things got steadily worse. It seemed to Marty that the only person having a good time was Rick, and she had serious doubts about him.

He couldn't understand the building hostility. The girls had been happy enough to see him at first. They should be glad that a major leaguer like himself would take the time to bother with a bunch of amateurs, he told himself, feeling self-righteous. And they shouldn't expect a person with so many demands on his time to be up on all the crazy rule variations of women's softball.

Glancing at his watch, he saw that it was almost time for an overseas call he'd been expecting. With a last wounded sigh, he turned to Marty.

"I have to go. We'll meet here tomorrow night, same time."

Marty just returned his gaze, unsmiling.

" 'Bye, girls," he called as he changed his shoes. "See you tomorrow."

Only two players returned his good-bye, but Rick didn't notice as he turned toward the parking lot. He had wanted to ask Marty to meet him later for a drink, but the expression on her face had stopped him cold. Girls usually *smiled* when they looked at him.

As soon as Rick was out of earshot, the players converged on Marty, all talking at once. Vicky and Pauline were outshouting each other, and even Betty was pulling impatiently at Marty's sleeve.

"Is he taking over the team?" Pauline asked.

"Is he *taken?*" Vicky demanded, batting her false eyelashes.

"He doesn't know what he's doing," someone else said.

"He's gorgeous."

"He's impossible."

"What a hunk."

"What a jerk!"

Marty's head began to throb. Just when she'd been revising her opinion of Rick for the better, some of the others were getting disillusioned.

"Marty, you've got to talk to him," Betty said quietly. "Or this team is going to fall apart."

Several of the more outspoken players agreed.

Marty's eyes widened with horror. Trying to broach this delicate subject with him would kill any chance of something personal developing between them. He'd never forgive her for puncturing his fragile male ego—again. She felt lucky that he didn't hold a grudge from the first time, even though she didn't understand why he didn't. She hadn't even decided if she wanted "something personal" between them, and already the chances of it ever happening were being obliterated.

"That's right, Marty," Pauline said loudly. "You

straighten him out or there's going to be nothing but trouble."

Marty nodded slowly. "You all be here tomorrow, same time," she said. "Rick won't come." She hesitated. "I promise."

She was caught right in the middle, and some little voice told her she was about to lose all the way around.

CHAPTER FOUR

Rick paced through the showroom, stopping once to wipe a smudge from the hood of a dark blue Seville, pausing again to eavesdrop on a young salesman moving in to close a deal. Rick had given up trying to make sense of the reports on his desk after staring unseeingly for almost an hour. It was unlike him to be so restless; usually he was able to concentrate under the most difficult circumstances.

He glanced up at the wall clock. The day was crawling by. He considered calling Marty, then discarded the idea. He could wait until turnout to see her. Perhaps they'd do something afterward.

He knew what he'd like to do, but she probably wouldn't go for that. Spending the weekend in bed on a first date was a *little* too much to hope for. Still . . . He shook his head with a private grin. If he kept thinking along those lines he'd have to sit behind his desk until he cooled off.

"Mr. Stokes, line one. Mr. Stokes, line one." Mavis's voice came clearly over the intercom.

He crossed to the receptionist's desk. "Who is it?" he asked the redhead.

"It's that Gibson woman who came in the other day," she said, voice disapproving. Rick knew that curiosity was eating at her, but Mavis was too much a professional to ask. One day he'd have to enlighten her, just to put her out of her misery.

"I'll get it in my office." He took the stairs two at a time.

Marty cleared her throat twice while she was on hold. What on earth was she going to say? Telling him that turnout had been postponed until Monday was the easy part; telling him not to be there wasn't. She'd have to go see him and try to explain it gently. She rubbed a throbbing temple, wishing it were someone else's job to break the news that he wasn't wanted at practice.

"Rick Stokes here." His deep voice reached through the telephone lines, carrying with it an image of his face.

She clutched the phone tighter. "This is Marty. I need to see you," she blurted. Nice lead in, real gentle.

There was a silence. "I'm glad to hear that," he drawled. "I need you too." If anything, his voice had deepened.

The only way to deal with his statement was to ignore it. "We have to talk about the team," she said, rapidly losing control of the conversation.

"I'd rather talk about us." There was laughter in his voice. Couldn't the man be serious for one minute?

"I'll come to your office," she said briskly. "What's a good time for you?"

"Can't it wait until turnout?"

"That's part of the news. Turnout has been postponed until Monday. Too many people had plans for this evening." She uncrossed and recrossed her legs, waiting nervously for his reaction.

"It has?" Quickly he thought over the situation. He usually didn't even come in on Saturdays and his afternoon was free.

"I'm busy all day," he said into the phone. "If you need to talk to me it will have to be over dinner."

"That's really not necessary," she said. "You must have a few moments—"

"I'm sorry. Did you have plans for this evening?"

At her negative reply, he continued briskly. "I'm tied up till six. We could go to an Italian place I know. It's quiet and we could talk there." He held his breath while she considered.

"I guess so," she said ungraciously. She didn't know which bothered her more, his suggestive comments or the businesslike way he handled the dinner invitation. "I really do need to see you," she admitted in a grumpy tone.

Damned if he knew why he bothered. He wasn't used to this type of treatment, or to resorting to all this scheming. But it would be worth it. If they didn't end up in bed tonight, they would eventually. He had confidence in himself and he knew that Marty wasn't totally immune. Just cautious.

"I'll pick you up at six thirty," he said, and hung up the phone, a sudden rush of irritation washing over him. It was about time he took control. Caution was one thing, but lack of appreciation something else.

Marty stared at the silent receiver. He'd hung up. He hadn't said good-bye or allowed her to speak. He'd just issued an order he expected her to follow and hung up. She slammed down the receiver, mad that she hadn't done it first. She wished he hadn't invited her to dinner just because she needed to talk to him. She wished she didn't have to. She wished that Rick Stokes was fat and ugly. She picked up a throw pillow and threw it.

Muttering, she walked across the living room, grabbed the pillow and tossed it back on the couch, not feeling one bit better. For the first time in memory, she wished that she'd never heard of the game of softball, and that she and Rick had a normal date.

Marty spent longer getting ready than she had for the high school prom. Discarded outfits lay on her bed in a heap. Earrings were scattered across her dresser and several pairs of shoes lay in the middle of the bedroom floor. At least her hair had cooperated and now curled away from her face and hung in golden waves to her shoulders.

She pulled on a silk dress with a floral pattern in soft pastels, fastened the narrow belt, fluffed out the full skirt, and eyed the scoop neckline. It revealed a hint of her high breasts, and made her feel deliciously feminine. With it she wore bone-colored heels that added two inches to her height and showcased her slender legs. She hoped the outfit wasn't too dressy.

Glancing at her watch, Marty saw that she was ready a half hour early. The apartment was clean, in case Rick stepped inside. Not that she expected to invite him in, but she liked to be prepared.

What she wasn't prepared for was the peal of the bell twenty minutes early and the bouquet of mixed flowers that greeted her when she opened the door. Rick was holding them, and he looked impressive in sport coat and tie. Marty's worry

64

that she had overdressed melted away as she stepped aside. He walked into her living room, filling it with his presence.

"I'm early," he apologized. "These are for you." Their hands touched as Marty reached for the flowers. Their gazes met and mingled for a long moment, then Rick pulled his hand away and Marty stepped back, reaching for the self-control that always seemed to elude her when he was around.

"They're beautiful," she murmured, savoring their sweet aroma. "Thank you." She moved toward the kitchen, then stopped. "I'll put them in water, and then we can go."

Rick waited tensely, half afraid he would lose his normally unfailing self-control if they lingered. Marty had been pretty wearing a uniform, but in a dress and heels she was breathtaking. It took every bit of his iron will to keep him from taking her in his arms.

When she was done with the flowers, he was waiting by the door, looking every inch the successful businessman in his charcoal slacks, blue shirt, and pearl-gray jacket. Marty noticed that his tie matched his eyes, and wondered if he'd done it on purpose. Probably.

All through dinner Marty pushed the food around on her plate and tried to formulate what she would say to Rick. She managed the right responses to his funny stories about life on the road with the Phantoms, and even answered a few questions about her job. When they'd finished dessert, she still hadn't managed to broach the subject that was uppermost in her thoughts.

"Would you like coffee?" Rick waited while Marty argued with herself. She just couldn't discuss his interference with the team in such a public place. Even though their table was secluded, she clutched at that as an excuse to stall for a few more minutes. Then, with a minimum of thought for the consequences, she was surprised to hear the words, "How about coffee at my place?" leave her mouth.

Rick didn't need to be asked twice. "Check please," he commanded, smiling across the table. Her suggestion was unexpected but not unwelcome. Quite the contrary.

Marty was a very special woman and he only wanted to convince her that it would be to their mutual enjoyment to spend time together. He didn't stop to analyze his feelings; he only knew that he wanted to feel his arms around her.

Before Marty had time to reconsider her rash offer, they were at her apartment door. She remembered the last time they'd been in that spot, with her nestled in his powerful arms, and a heated blush swept over her cheeks and warmed her whole body. She was tempted to plead a headache and slip inside alone, but that would cancel the whole purpose of their dinner. She had to talk to him and it had to be now.

While Marty made coffee, her ears strained for sounds from the other room. The first notes of a dreamy Kenny Rogers ballad drifted into the kitchen. When she returned with the coffee, she noticed that he'd removed his jacket and loosened the blue tie. The sleeves of his pale shirt were turned back, revealing powerful forearms. Big hands took the tray she had planned to set on the table between the couch and a chair, placing it instead on the coffee table.

Marty had no choice but to sit beside him. She

busied herself with the coffee things while he waited, only breaking the quiet between them to request his coffee black.

"You have a varied music collection," he said. "I saw a few of my own favorites." He accepted the mug she offered, then set it back down.

"We have a lot in common, Marty." The words tickled her ear as he slid his arm across the back of the couch.

She sipped the hot beverage, burning her tongue in the process. Her trembling hands gripped the mug. She stared at a vase of flowers rather than the man next to her. The song ended and she could hear his breathing. It sounded shallow. She took another sip, further injuring her mouth, as Kenny began to sing about cowards and bullies.

"I can't wait any longer," she blurted, setting down the mug.

Rick's eyes glittered as his arm curled around her shoulders. "I'm glad to hear that," he said, his voice a husky rasp. "I can't wait either."

Rick's head lowered and Marty's lips parted in a sigh. Then she remembered why they were here and she jerked away.

Her action so surprised Rick that she'd managed to slip from his embrace before he knew what was happening. "What—"

"Stop!" she exclaimed.

Her agitation was like icy water to his ardor.

"What on earth did you think I was going to do?" he asked as he reached for his coffee cup. "Go for the vein in your neck?" His cheeks were a dull red beneath their tan.

"I'm sorry," Marty said, feeling silly. "But we have to talk."

Rick knew what was coming. She certainly had a one-track mind. "All right," he agreed, resigned. "I know that there's been something bothering you. Are you worried about uniforms, hotel reservations, what?"

Marty blinked in confusion. She hadn't given any of that a thought. The tournament was getting closer all the time and there were arrangements to be made.

"I'll get sizes Monday night," he continued. "I've already spoken to a manufacturer who is sure he can get new uniforms done before we leave."

"We?"

"Of course. I have a sister in Seattle, remember? It will give me a chance to visit her."

Oh, Lord. It hadn't occurred to her that he might accompany them. A nightmare vision of him chewing out the team in front of five thousand fans passed before her eyes.

"I thought you weren't interested in amateur sports," she said, twisting her hands and trying to force her brain to work. She was still recovering from Rick's potent charm, and conniving was a tall order. "Women's sports are so, uh, slow moving after the big time."

His brows drew together in a frown.

"I mean," she continued, trying to sound nonchalant, "you're so busy with your business and all. Surely you don't really have the time to get involved with us."

He leaned back against the cushions, studying her. "What's going on?" he asked. "Since we are *both athletes*, you can level with me."

Marty's gaze dropped away from his as he threw her words back at her. He was right. Her efforts not to mess things up between the two of them were only making it all worse. The attraction she felt toward him had to be put aside while she dealt with this other problem. Perhaps if she didn't look directly into those clear, sexy dark eyes, ignored the way his voice raised goose bumps on her skin she would be able to manage.

"The team doesn't want you at turnout anymore," she said boldly. "You're too, uh, disruptive."

Rick absently tugged at the fringe on one of the throw pillows. He couldn't believe the girls would feel that way after he'd tried to help them. He didn't understand what the problem was, but had no intention of being barred from his own team's practices. Or being prevented from spending as much time as possible with Marty. He was determined to possess her. Nothing else would satisfy the hunger building within him. His mind worked furiously as his fingers traced the words, *Atlantic City,* embroidered on the pillow.

Marty watched him in tense silence, acutely aware of the allure of his full lips. She expected an argument; instead he appeared to be considering her request, his dark brows pulled together. This might be easy, she thought after a moment, pouring herself more coffee with hands that trembled only slightly. After all, Rick's a reasonable adult, and one who wouldn't care to force himself in where he wasn't wanted. He has too many other interests. He'll just . . .

"Disruptive in what way?"

So much for reasonable.

"Maybe if you studied the handbook," she suggested, "really got familiar with the rules. Then next fall—"

"Next fall? Are you saying I should go off in a

corner, read the book and write expense checks? That I need months of preparation to help with the team?" His voice was getting louder, but he wasn't actually shouting. Yet.

Marty winced at his stormy expression. "Well, what I'm saying is that Pat and some of the others may, uh, quit if you show up again." The last few words were mumbled. She stared down at her full cup, held tightly in her hands.

Rick had to bend forward to hear her. "Don't worry about it," he said suddenly. "No one is going to quit."

Her head jerked up. "You'll stay away from turn-out?" she asked hastily setting the cup aside.

"Nope." He lifted his hand to tangle his fingers in the soft strands of her hair. Marty's whole scalp tingled under his light caress.

"But, Rick . . ." She remembered her rash promise to the others.

His arm once again dropped to her shoulders. "Trust me," he murmured, staring hotly at her mouth. "It will all work out."

"But . . ." she managed before his head came down and she forgot what she'd been about to say. Trust him, her heart encouraged, or maybe it was her hormones talking. He *was* virile and sexy and wonderfully male.

Follow your instincts and discover the magic he's offering, she tried to tell herself. A stray doubt niggled in the back of her mind, but she had no time to examine it.

"Enough talk," he whispered as he pulled her firmly toward him.

He leaned closer, thick lashes screening his blue eyes. Much bluer than his tie, she thought, just before his mouth touched her own.

The pressure was gentle and sweet as his mouth moved on hers, her hands fluttered against his chest, then slid up the smooth fabric of his shirt and circled his neck. She could feel his arms tightening around her even as his lips parted a fraction.

"Sweet," he murmured. "Sweet Marty." A shudder went through his strong body. Then his mouth again claimed hers as his tightly held control slipped one more notch.

The last shreds of constraint were ripping away from Marty, revealing a passion she'd never before felt. It seemed so right that Rick was the one to expose that side of her nature.

Rick's eyes were dark with passion and there was a flush across his cheek bones as he leaned over her heated body. His mouth looked softer, fuller than before. How she hated to stop the delicious onslaught he was waging against her defenses. It was almost more than she could do. But, sensing that involvement on her side could easily go far beyond mere lust, Marty managed to pull away.

When Rick felt her stiffen, he stilled. His intention hadn't been to rush her, but his body craved the exquisite fulfillment he knew he would find with her. Reluctantly, he sat up, helping her to a sitting position before raising one of her hands to his mouth, his eyes glittering dangerously.

"I need you, Marty," he said softly, placing a kiss in the palm. "You're very special to me." His chest rose and fell with a shuddering breath.

She shook her head. "It's too soon to be special."

He sighed, kissing each of her knuckles in turn, knowing he couldn't convince her otherwise. The only way to do that was to wait. With hindsight she would see.

71

A tremor coursed through her as his lips brushed the back of her hand, a final caress before lifting his head. Already she regretted stopping the magic that had flowered between them, but was relieved when he rose to go.

It was much later when she realized she'd failed to extract his promise to skip turnout. But that was the least of her worries as she tossed and turned through much of the night.

Marty resisted the urge to miss practice herself. Caution might be a part of her nature, but cowardice wasn't. She had to go, if only to see how upset the others would be at her failure to detour their nemesis.

When she arrived, no one asked how the talk with Rick had gone. She began to warm up with Pauline while the other players went through their various individual routines of stretching, jogging, and playing catch. Marty's gaze kept straying to the parking lot past the trees, and then Pauline called her name sharply.

"You're going to get one in the ear if you don't pay attention. What's bothering you?" the catcher said, after the ball narrowly missed Marty's head.

"Nothing," she lied, glancing once again at the nearly empty lot. Perhaps he'd reconsidered. Surely a man like Rick Stokes didn't have to go where he wasn't wanted. The team practice was probably the only place in Allentown where he wasn't welcome. There and at the Lincoln dealership out toward Bethlehem.

"I guess you took care of Stokes," Pauline continued, closing the gap between them, watching the black Mercedes pull up.

"I guess I sure did," Marty echoed glumly.

All action on the field ceased abruptly as a shrill

72

whistle pierced the early evening air. Marty's mouth fell open with surprise as Rick then raised one arm, beckoning them. Not waiting to see if they would respond, he opened the trunk of the Mercedes, then leaned nonchalantly against the car's side.

Pauline looked at Marty. "What's he up to?" she asked. "Did he blow a dog whistle?"

"I don't think so," Marty answered, glaring across the field. Within her, a hunger to see him again warred briefly with dread. Hunger won. "I don't think he'll go away until we see what he wants."

Vicky, Betty, and several of the others, with Pat in the lead, were already jogging across the field. Rick waited patiently, wearing a self-satisfied grin.

"Come on," Pauline grumbled. "We might as well get this over with."

Marty dragged her feet. Perhaps if she were careful to stay in back, she wouldn't be blamed for the lynching. "Remember, he's our sponsor," she called. But no one gave any indication of having heard as they advanced on the car.

Marty's steps slowed even more. Pauline didn't notice as she moved briskly to catch up. By the time Marty reached the car, the other women were gathered around the open trunk, laughing and chattering as if Rick were once again their idol.

Looking up, he moved toward Marty, his expression growing serious. Their eyes met and held.

"How are you?" he questioned, his hand rising and then dropping back to his side. "Been sleeping okay?"

Marty's head bobbed as she gazed up at his face,

73

lingering on each strong feature. She'd actually sent this man away.

On closer inspection she saw that the lines fanning out from his eyes were etched deeper than before and his eyes themselves were red-rimmed. Had he spent wakeful nights thinking of her?

For the first time she noticed what dangled from his other hand and her eyes widened. No wonder her teammates were acting as if he'd never been banned.

She looked past him and saw more reasons for their good humor, fifteen of them if she guessed correctly. Where had Rick Stokes managed to get his hands on equipment bags in the team colors with PENNSYLVANIA lettered neatly on the sides— at a moment's notice yet? And how had he known just the right method to insure his welcome back into the fold? The man was a born manipulator!

Thinking of the other evening, Marty flushed to the roots of her hair. Thank goodness things hadn't gone any further than they had.

Everyone enthused over the new bags a few minutes longer, then returned to the diamond. Everyone but Marty.

"Where'd you get 'em?" she asked as soon as her teammates were out of earshot. "It takes weeks to have anything printed this late in the season."

"I know." His grin was smug; his eyes twinkled.

"Your bribery really worked," she said with a rueful smile. "They've forgotten all about the other night."

"I know," he repeated. "Would bribery work with you?" he quizzed, head cocked to one side. "Two bags perhaps? A new jacket?" His voice was teasing. "I've got it!" he exclaimed, slapping the car's hood with his palm. "How about shoes? Pitchers always need shoes. White with blue laces."

Marty swung the empty vinyl tote he'd given her at his head and he retreated, laughing.

"You fiend! Proud of yourself, aren't you?" She glanced over at the field, where the others had resumed practice, then back at the man who'd circled behind the car, arms protecting his head. "What are you getting us the next time you put both feet in your mouth, Stokes? Hooded sweat shirts?"

"Batting helmets," he said, still chuckling. "And one for the sponsor."

She hadn't noticed that, while they'd been trading insults, he'd come back around the car. Before she could object, his large hands grabbed her upper arms and he hauled her against his wide chest.

"Gotcha."

Marty wiggled in protest, but if truth be known she would have been disappointed had he let her go. The expression on his face was predatory as his head lowered. She expected a brief, simple kiss, considering the proximity of the rest of the players, but he surprised her once again.

The kiss was neither brief nor simple. She thought her feet left the ground at some point, but couldn't be sure. His tongue seared the tender flesh inside her mouth like flame, probing, dominating, claiming, shattering her. When he finally pulled away, her lips felt bruised. All the blood in her body seemed to be rushing to the core.

Rick's eyes had darkened nearly to black, and a tremor rippled through him. His arms fell away and he took a step back, studying Marty. His reaction to her was part excitement and part puzzlement, the reaction of an overheated youth rather

75

than a man who'd been to the city and back more than once. What had started as a challenge was rapidly turning into something much more complicated.

"I know what you want," he rasped. "It's the same thing I want, and it's not blue sweats or new shoes." He slammed down the trunk lid and turned toward the field, an equipment bag in one hand. "Be careful what you wish for, little girl," he taunted over his shoulder. "You just might get it."

CHAPTER FIVE

After changing shoes, stowing cleats and mitt in her new equipment bag, Marty straightened and glanced toward the parking area. Much as she hated to face Rick, given his parting remark before turnout, curiosity propelled her forward.

His presence during practice hadn't seemed to bother anyone but herself. Everyone gradually relaxed and seemed to forget he was there—everyone except Marty.

Rick had stayed on the sidelines and kept quiet, except for a couple of conferences with the coach. Marty had noticed that Pat turned to him during batting practice when one of the players was having problems. After helping, Rick went docilely back to the sidelines.

Marty was unable to block his earlier remarks from her mind, and she wondered what the others were thinking about the kiss they must have seen. Not able to concentrate, she managed to make enough dumb mistakes for all of them. Several times she'd glanced over to where Rick stood to see whether he noticed. If anything, he appeared to be daydreaming. Being there and not taking over must have been a terrific strain to his male ego, but he managed to keep his mouth shut until Pat called time.

She got a list of uniform sizes from the players and handed it to Rick. After praising their efforts, mentioning several players by name, he left amid a renewed chorus of thank-you's for the bags.

Marty was glad that everyone was busy talking about the prospect of new uniforms for the Nationals. No one commented on her performance either before or during practice.

Now she felt that Rick deserved to hear what a good job he'd done, since she had been the one to tell him when he was disruptive and unwanted. Getting the new bags had only gotten his foot back in the door; it was his effort to change his attitude that kept the door open long enough for the others to accept his presence again.

Marty shook her head as she walked toward his car. Where on earth had he gotten those bags? The man was either a genius, or a damned handsome con artist.

Where the bags came from was her first question when she got to him.

He smiled down at her, cocking a dark eyebrow. "Feminine curiosity is a powerful force, isn't it?" he taunted as he leaned against the side of the black car and studied her. "I wondered if it would bug you so much you'd have to speak to me again." He jammed his hands into the pockets of his jeans, straining the soft, faded material across his flat, very masculine body.

Marty's gaze darted away from his tight, sexy jeans, only to collide with the knowing look in his blue eyes. Damn the man for being so aware of her reactions. She scuffed the dusty ground with the toe of her worn tennis shoe. He was insufferable when he was feeling smug.

"Are you going to tell me?" she asked. "Or are you just going to stand there and gloat?"

He leaned forward, and instinctively she took a step back.

"Gloating can be kind of fun," he murmured, voice a throaty purr. "Why don't you come over to my house. I promise to let you gloat all you want after you've had your way with me."

Marty burst out laughing at his outrageous words. The man was impossible. "Tell me how you got those bags so quickly," she said, pausing for effect. "And I might consider your suggestion."

His eyes widened, and then his face took on a wounded expression. "You're playing with me," he said, sounding hurt.

No, but I'd like to, she realized before the thought could be censored. It was true. She *would* like to. Rick Stokes would be a wonderful lover, a once-in-a-lifetime experience, but the whole idea was impossible. She'd never been one to leap indiscriminately, and she wasn't going to start with Allentown's celebrity jock.

Rick watched the emotions play across her face, and became serious. His hand closed around her elbow to prevent her from retreating any farther. "Come by for a drink and I'll share my secret with you," he suggested, watching her gray eyes closely.

"That's not a good idea. I don't play those games."

He was sorry to see that the smile had left her eyes, leaving them more silver than smoky, and much less easy to read. "I wasn't playing," he denied, releasing his hold on her arm. "A drink and an explanation, that's all it will be. You could check out the house and see if you think it would be suitable for a party I'm giving." The idea had just come to him, but it was a good one.

"Party?" she frowned. Why did he need her opinion for that? She didn't travel in his social circle; she imagined he invited the top brass of Allentown when he entertained.

"I want to give the team a reception to kick off our trip," he explained. "Let's talk about it over something tall and cool. My tongue's hanging out."

He grinned to himself. It's a good thing she didn't know how true that last statement was or she'd *run* all the way to Seattle. He'd already discovered that Marty was different from the other women he knew. At first he thought she was playing hard to get, but now he wasn't so sure. What surprised him was that he'd bet a share in the dealership that she was attracted to him, yet she still rebuffed him at every turn. Even though he respected her attitude, even grudgingly admired it, he wasn't above using every persuasive tool he could to help his own cause.

Usually women fell into his bed with little effort on his part. Sometimes the effort came in trying to keep them out—but not Marty. She intrigued him, and he was beginning to realize that getting her into bed was only a small part of what he wanted. *That* thought was almost enough to make *him* run all the way to Seattle.

"Are you coming?" he asked gruffly when he realized Marty was staring at him.

She shook her head, and realized that it was with real regret. She'd heard that his house, built two years before in the most exclusive section of

80

town, was quite a showplace. If Jerry hadn't been expecting her to meet him for pizza, she might have agreed.

And there was another reason to hesitate. Marty would have had to be blind to miss the lust that flared in Rick's eyes. He wanted her. She'd known that all along, ignoring it because that was easier than dealing with it. What was harder to ignore was the fact that she wanted him too. So perhaps it would be best if she only saw him when she had to. After Nationals he'd be returning to whatever he did with his time. If she wasn't careful, when the season was over for him, she'd be left picking up pieces.

"I can't go," she said. "I'm meeting a friend for dinner and I'm already late."

"Dressed like that?" he exclaimed in disbelief, indicating her sweat pants and faded T-shirt.

Marty's chin jutted out at his skepticism. "Like this," she said.

Rick realized that he'd made her angry. "Well, another time," he said. "I've got a salmon stowed in the freezer. I'll barbecue it, if you like salmon?" He ended on a questioning note.

"That would be wonderful," she admitted, forgetting her resolution of only moments before. "Meanwhile, won't you tell me about the bags?"

"I guess I won't have any peace until I do," he said with an exaggerated sigh. "I called every soccer coach I know, and several I don't. With their season not starting till fall, I was able to persuade one from Lancaster to sell me his bags and order more for his own players."

Marty's eyes grew soft. "That was a great thing for you to do," she said. He watched her full mouth closely.

"Then how about a reward?" he asked, leaning forward. "A little kiss to take away the sting?"

Marty pulled back. "Goodness is it's own reward," she said primly.

He glowered. "I shouldn't have told you."

"Why not?"

"You kissed me when you thought I wasn't so nice." The teasing light was back in his eyes.

She could feel her cheeks heating up. She'd blushed more since she'd met Rick than during her whole adolescence. Groping for a new subject, she asked about the party.

"We'll have it this Friday, the night before we leave for Seattle," he said in answer to her query. "The girls can bring their families and I'll ask a sports writer I know, the softball commissioner . . . Now do I get a reward?" he asked, his grin deepening the lines that fanned out from his eyes.

"No," she answered, unable to prevent herself from smiling back at him. "I'll let you know when."

"Is there anyone else I should invite?"

Marty gave him the names of the team's former sponsor and several loyal fans who'd attended most of their games, and he wrote them in a small notebook.

Marty glanced at her watch. "I have to run," she said. "I'm really late now."

She waved as she drove from the lot. Rick was still standing there, and he was scowling.

Marty's mind was busy scheming as she drove to the pizza place to meet Jerry. He worked out at Pauline's gym and saw her almost every day, but Pauline had confided in Marty that Jerry treated her like one of the fixtures. Rick's party would be an ideal opportunity for Jerry to see the young catcher in an entirely different light.

Marty stopped at a pay phone and cleared her plan with Pauline before continuing on to the restaurant. Jerry didn't stand a chance.

When she asked him over pizza to escort her to the reception, he hesitated. Parties were not his forte, but a little pleading on her part convinced him she'd be lost without a date. The reminder that he would get to meet Rick Stokes was all the additional push he needed.

Marty didn't usually interfere so blatantly in the lives of others, but she liked Jerry and Pauline. Besides, Pauline had convinced her that she and Jerry were perfect for each other. Feeling generous, Marty split the bill with Jerry and headed home. Tomorrow promised to be a hectic one at work and she needed to get some rest.

The next few days were spent doing as many greenhouse installations as possible, shopping for a slicker and a new umbrella to protect her from the Seattle rain she'd been warned about, and practicing with the team. Before Marty had a chance to catch her breath, the day of Rick's party arrived.

The players were all excited about it, even Louise who wasn't going to Seattle. Pat had picked up another pitcher for the trip, but Marty wished Louise's husband would let her go.

Marty vowed that no husband of hers would ever tell her what to do. It would be an equal partnership all the way. That was one more reason to avoid Rick Stokes. He probably didn't consider women partners in any but the most basic activities. Just because he'd done a complete turnabout at practice, helping only when he was asked and giving encouragement instead of criticism, didn't mean he'd changed his spots.

Marty's father was attending the party, but he'd declined a lift with Jerry and herself. As she studied her reflection in the mirror and fastened gold-filigreed earrings, she shrugged. If he wanted to go alone, it was his choice. She was surprised he was going at all.

When Jerry arrived to pick her up, he admired Marty's brand new aqua-chiffon dress.

"I brought you this," he said, presenting her with a flawless gardenia and blushing beneath his tan.

Not for the first time, she wondered why Jerry was so shy. He was usually at ease around her, but she could feel his tension tonight. It was apparent that he was only going to the party for her sake. She pinned the flower into her hair, thanking him.

"You look great," she said sincerely, admiring the beige knit shirt that emphasized his broad shoulders and tapered torso. It was a perfect contrast to his tanned skin and blue eyes, and teamed well with the ivory slacks that hugged his lean hips and long legs. Marty hoped that Pauline would be able to make a dent in Jerry's shyness before he got the mistaken impression that Marty herself was interested in him.

"Do you, uh, think that Pauline will be at the party?" he asked as they drove across town.

The tone of his voice was offhand, so Marty was surprised to see that his knuckles were white where he gripped the steering wheel.

"I think she will," Marty answered nonchalantly, resisting the urge to clap. "She said something about going with Vicky because neither of them had dates."

"Oh." Marty saw Jerry's hands relax on the wheel and she smiled to herself.

"Don't feel you have to stick with me," she told him. "Once we're inside I'll have plenty of people to talk to."

"Is it because of Rick that you didn't want to go alone?" Jerry asked suddenly, slowing to turn onto a tree-lined street.

Marty was surprised at the question. "Why do you ask that?" The defensiveness in her voice made her wince.

"Is it?" he persisted.

"Of course not. I just hate to walk alone into a room full of people."

"You could have gone with Pauline and Vicky," he pointed out reasonably.

Marty was saved from a reply when they pulled into the driveway of a large multilevel house set back from the road. There were cars all around and the double doors at the top of the steps were thrown open. Although the house was obviously new, brick trim and careful landscaping made it blend into the neighborhood.

Until Jerry's question, Marty had managed to keep her mind stuck on getting him and Pauline together. Now thoughts of seeing Rick again intruded, and she trembled. Despite all her sensible resolutions, she'd still had her hair done in soft curls atop her head, and spent more than she intended on the new dress.

It seemed that whenever she was around Rick, she was wearing sweats and a T-shirt. Tonight she meant to change the impression that she always dressed like a bag lady. Of course none of it had anything to do with any attraction she felt for Stokes. It was strictly impersonal. Her nails dug into her small silver purse as Jerry escorted her up the steps.

Rick was standing inside the doorway, talking to Gordon Gibson and Vera Flowers when Marty and Jerry walked in. Marty was so startled to see her father with Vera that she completely missed the expression on Rick's face when he saw Jerry at her elbow.

Rick had offered to pick Marty up when he called to give her the time of the party. Somehow, even though she had declined, he assumed she knew he wanted her to spend the evening with him.

Now, as he stood greeting his guests, blue eyes shooting daggers at Marty's date, Rick replayed their phone conversation in his head. It was only then that he realized he hadn't made his intentions clear. From the husky quality of Marty's voice over the phone, he'd gotten the impression that she wanted to be with him, but he realized now that it was only his own overactive imagination at work. If the young blond hunk standing next to her was what Marty found exciting in a man, Rick didn't stand a chance.

The guy had to be younger than the twenty-five years she had confessed to, and he looked like a beachboy in the snug tan shirt, his well-developed muscles bulging and flexing with every breath.

Suddenly Rick felt old. Old and boringly conventional with his neatly trimmed hair, gold cuff links, and silk tie.

If Rick was impressed with Marty's new hairstyle or the way she was dressed, he didn't show it. Rick's blue eyes were cold and there was a set smile on his rugged face as she introduced him to Jerry. If his greeting was less than warm, Jerry's response more than made up for it. It was clear that he was impressed by the retired athlete.

"You used to be one of my heroes," Jerry told him enthusiastically as he pumped Rick's hand. "I watched you play with the Phantoms when I was a kid. My dad and I never missed a home game."

Rick's smile seemed to stiffen. Marty couldn't understand his attitude. When he'd called to offer her a ride she'd thought for a moment he was asking her to be his date. Then she'd decided he was just being polite. She looked around now to see who was with him, but the only other people in the large entry hall were Marty's father and Vera Flowers.

Marty smiled to herself. For a crazy moment she'd thought they'd come together. What a silly idea. Vera walked through to the living room, greeting friends, and Gordon turned to Marty and Jerry.

"Hi, Dad," she greeted as Rick moved to welcome someone else.

"Martha, Jerry." Mr. Gibson nodded to them both. "You look very pretty this evening," he told Marty.

Her eyes widened with surprise. "Why, thank you. You look very handsome yourself." As the unaccustomed compliment left her mouth, she realized it was true. There was something different about her father. Marty's eyes narrowed as she attempted to study him closer, but he stepped away.

"I'll see you both later," he said over his shoulder.

As he went across the entry hall into the vast living room, it came to her. He was wearing a stylish sport coat and well-tailored slacks, both obviously new. The trendy outfit made him look younger.

The party was progressing nicely when Rick managed to break away from a group of people discussing the current season's Phantom team. His gaze had been seeking out Marty again and again. Each time he'd seen her she had been with that blond hunk. Playing the jovial host while seething inwardly was beginning to unravel the edges of his cool demeanor. What he wanted to do was to throw her over his shoulder and tell everyone else, golden boy included, to go home.

He moved slightly away from the nearest knot of laughing men and women. Visions of Marty's slim, pliant body sprawled on the carpet of his den, her skin reflecting the flames from the stone fireplace, made his own body harden in response. As his lips curved upward into a lusty grin, he saw Marty lean forward and whisper something into Jerry's ear. Rick's fingers tightened on his glass and his eyes narrowed into a murderous glare.

If Jerry was what she wanted, he finally decided as he consciously loosened his grip on the etched crystal, the least he could do was to make sure the younger man treated her right. A bitter taste filled Rick's mouth, and he took a swallow of his drink. He had the impression that Jerry wasn't all that interested in Marty. When her attention was elsewhere, Rick saw him looking around as if searching for someone. Unable to stay away, Rick was on his way to ask her to dance when the local head of the Big Brothers organization stopped him. By the time he had extricated himself, Marty was dancing with Jerry.

Rick altered his direction and asked Vera Flowers to dance instead. When Marty's father cut in,

Rick again searched the room for Marty. She was nowhere in sight, but Jerry was dancing to a slow song with the catcher, Pauline, who had just arrived. Despite his own jealousy, Rick didn't like the way Jerry's cheek rested on her hair and the way he held her. What if Marty saw them? She'd be hurt for sure.

The thought brought forth a fierce protectiveness in Rick. He checked the kitchen, the rec room, where several of his guests were playing pool, and the patio. Giving up, he returned to the living room. This time Marty was there, talking with great animation to Vicky and several other members of the team. Rick knew it was only a brave front. Pauline and Jerry had disappeared.

She'd noticed that her date was missing, and the dear, courageous girl was putting on one hell of an act. God, she was beautiful with her hair up like that, even if her interest in Jerry was totally ridiculous and misguided. The cool blue of the dress made her skin seem rosy and her eyes enormous.

Pausing for one pain-filled glance, Rick renewed his search for Marty's date. He wasn't sure what he'd do when he found Jerry, but throwing him in the outdoor pool seemed like a good idea.

Tearing his gaze away, he slipped outdoors. Perhaps he could persuade the punk to return to Marty's side. Rick's hands balled into fists as he resisted the idea of pounding on the little creep. If Pauline was still with him, Rick would insist she go back in and dance. That would separate her from Marty's date with the least embarrassment to anyone.

When Rick found the young couple, he realized it would take more than a dance request to separate them. More like a shoehorn or a crowbar.

Jerry and Pauline were almost fully concealed in the shade of a large tree beside the pool, locked in each other's arms. Furious at Jerry's defection, Rick backed away, frustrated. He wasn't sure he could have spoken without punching Jerry's lights out, and he realized that a fistfight would only call attention to the younger man's shameless abandonment of his date.

Righteous anger hardened Rick's features as he stalked to where Marty stood talking to an older couple Rick had seen frequently at the ball field.

"Let's dance," he said, his voice grating as he took her hand before she had time to accept or decline.

Marty resisted, trying to pull loose. "I don't care to dance now," she retorted, twisting her arm. He'd been ignoring her half the evening and she had no intention of doing what he so imperiously commanded.

Rick paid no attention to her protests, dragging her stiffened body to the section of the room where four or five couples swayed in one another's arms. Marty stumbled as she tried to dig her spike heels into the unyielding tile. He kept moving despite repeated jerks of her imprisoned arm and the stream of insulting names she uttered just loud enough for him to hear. From the color that ran up his cheeks, she knew he heard her muttered abuse. Short of screaming or kicking him in the shins, there didn't seem to be any way to dissuade him.

Wishing the number on the stereo were a fast-paced rock song instead of a dreamy ballad by Ronnie Milsap, Marty glared, hands on hips, as Rick held out his arms. An expression she would have described as pain crossed his face before she sighed deeply and allowed him to gather her close. The heat radiating from him made her tremble all over as she melted against him. His sharp intake of breath stilled any further protests she might have made, and he pulled her even closer, despite the other couples' interested stares.

"I love your new hairdo," he murmured into her ear. "It makes me want to take the pins out, one by one."

Marty was trying hard to stay angry at the way he'd railroaded her onto the dance floor. Instead, her annoyance melted away and she gave herself up to the bliss of being close against him. The party sounds and sights faded away as they held each other and gently swayed.

She was thinking that she had Rick all wrong and then he spoke, shattering his shiny new image into fragments.

"I hope you appreciate the way I rescued you," he said, still annoyed with her for coming to the party with someone else. "When it comes to men, your taste is in your shoes." As soon as the words left his lips, Rick realized they didn't convey quite what he meant.

Before he had time to add anything else, Marty stiffened and stepped back. The arrogance in his expression, added to his other transgressions, brought her temper to flash point. First he failed to make her his date for the party, then he manhandled her, and now he insulted her.

"You're right," she muttered past clenched teeth, acutely aware of the people all around them. "I sure as hell can't choose men. Look at the one I'm dancing with."

Rick winced, noticing that two of the other couples were looking at them with curiosity. Sensing that the discussion was going downhill fast, he suggested they retreat to the patio.

"I have nothing else to say to you," Marty snapped.

"You'd better stick with me," Rick answered in a stage whisper. "You've already been dumped by one escort." As soon as the words were out, he felt remorseful. That was really hitting below the belt.

To his surprise, Marty looked puzzled at first, and then a wide smile flashed across her face. "You mean that it worked?" she squeaked, hands digging into his upper arms.

"Worked? Your date is outside necking with your catcher, that's what I mean." A dark flush colored his cheeks as he realized how loudly he'd spoken.

"Damn," he muttered. "I'm sorry, Marty." He dragged her from the circle of eavesdroppers and down the hall to his study. Shutting the door behind them, he turned to the now chuckling female he had expected to dissolve into tears of humiliation.

"You did say you saw Jerry and Pauline together, didn't you?" she asked eagerly, grabbing his sleeve in excitement. "Kissing?"

Rick nodded, slightly dazed. Hiding a broken heart was one thing, but Marty's reaction was excessive. Perhaps he should slap her cheek? Lightly, of course.

Before he could decide what to do, Marty threw her arms around his neck. Instinctively, his hands clamped her slim waist. "Do you have any idea how long I've schemed to get those two together?" she asked, leaning back so she could look into his face.

Rick shook his head, bewildered.

"How can some people be so blind, so stupid, so just plain dumb?" she continued, talking more to herself than to him. She had pulled away, gesturing with one hand.

Rick decided it was time for him to regain control of the situation. "I don't know," he said firmly. "I don't know how some people can miss what's right in front of their noses. Suppose you tell me, before I kiss the breath out of you."

Marty's eyes focused on him again. *"What?"* He had her complete attention now.

"Did you come to the party with that surf bum just so he'd meet Pauline here?" Rick asked, curiosity delaying his intentions of kissing her breathless.

"He's not a surf bum, he's a body-builder," Marty explained. "Jerry and Pauline have known each other for a year. He works out at her gym."

Rick nodded. "I see. And how do you know him?" he asked.

"I work with him."

"What do you mean?" Rick demanded. He didn't like the sound of that.

Marty laughed again, a chortle as bubbly as champagne. "He works at Gibson Enterprises. We crew together to install the greenhouses."

"Good Lord," Rick muttered, the pieces finally falling into place. After a moment he said, "I have one more question."

"Fire away," Marty invited as he stepped forward and once more wrapped his arms around her.

"What's this beach bum mean to you?"

"Body-builder," she corrected him, her pulse racing at his nearness.

"Whatever."

"He's a friend."

"That's all?"

"That's all."

"Good," he said softly as he lowered his head.

Marty's breath stopped in her throat. The small flame that had been burning deep within her, growing brighter and hotter the longer she stood so close to Rick, burst into a raging inferno. When his mouth covered hers, she opened it to welcome him. Rick's arms pulled her against his big body, and his tongue plunged past her soft lips to sweep into every corner of the moist cavern beyond. Marty's nostrils flared, drawing in the spice of Rick's cologne and the underlying clean aroma of his warm flesh. Her legs trembled as her tongue touched his, entwined briefly, then darted away. Her daring brought a rumble of response from deep in his throat as his grip tightened and his mouth jerked away from hers.

Marty moaned in protest, seeking his mouth once more, but he began to drop feathery teasing kisses on her closed eyes, her cheeks, her brows. Finally, the tip of his tongue traced the outer curve of her ear, before his mouth returned to hers.

He murmured something unintelligible, the words floating around Marty like wisps of smoke, before his lips took hers in a heady show of driving male power. The assault hovered somewhere between pleasure and pain as his tongue mastered hers. Marty's fingers tightened in his hair as his hand slid to the curve of her breast.

Rick's other hand skimmed down her spine and settled on one softly rounded hip, pulling her against the evidence of his arousal. "God, you feel good," he muttered.

"Mmmm," was all Marty could manage in reply as she buried her face into the heated skin at his throat. Her breast pushed into his open hand and her insides turned to liquid as she pressed against him. After another hot searing kiss, he rested his chin against her shoulder, his chest rising and falling rapidly. Marty's own breath was quick and shallow as her heart began to quiet and the fog in her brain slowly cleared.

"You're wonderful," he murmured, pulling a long, deep breath into his lungs. "Unselfish, smart, beautiful, brave, graceful." He swallowed and continued, laughter beginning to thread its way through the deep voice. "Feisty, scheming, conniving . . ."

Marty pulled away as soon as she realized what he was saying. "What about you?" she protested. "Arrogant, chauvinistic, bossy, conceited."

"Conceited?" His eyebrows rose.

"You agree with the rest then?" she asked, trying to ignore the way his navy-blue gaze was affecting her knees.

"Hmm, what was it you said? Handsome, intelligent, virile . . . Let's see if I can remember how you described me at the ball park that day. You said something about my rear end, if I recall." He scratched his chin methodically.

Marty flushed. He really had overheard her!

His voice tapered off as their gazes locked. The silence in the room became louder than any blaring trumpet. When his eyes looked to Marty's mouth, she felt a slow pulsating begin in a thousand nerve endings. The primitive rhythm was converging at her deepest center.

His head was dipping once again when voices

from the hallway reminded them both that there was a party going on beyond the closed door.

"Let's send them all home," he whispered. "We'll have our own party."

Marty was breathless in answering. "Sorry, but I have a plane to catch." She knew Rick had heard the regret in her voice by the tightening of his grip. "It's a nice party," she added. "I think everyone is having a good time."

"Especially Pauline and that beachboy you brought," Rick said. "But it would have been a better party if the new uniforms had arrived on time. I was really looking forward to passing them out tonight."

"I don't think anyone really minded not getting them. It would have been nice, but you know how superstitious ball players can be. Changing uniforms during a winning streak might have been disastrous," Marty said in a serious voice.

"You don't believe that drivel, do you?" Rick's voice was incredulous.

"Don't you?" she asked. "Didn't you ever perform some little ritual before you went up to the plate? Or carry a rabbit's foot in your pocket?"

"Naw." He hesitated and his cheeks grew pink. "Unless you'd count wearing my lucky socks," he added in a low voice.

"Lucky socks?" Marty's eyes began to twinkle. "I hope you weren't one of those guys who believed that washing them would break your hitting streak."

"God, no. But the trainer did complain about having to darn them for me when they started to wear out. After a while they got so thin I wore them over another pair. They still seemed to work," he said proudly.

Studying the expression on his face, Marty wasn't sure that he was telling the truth about his lucky socks. "I have to go," she murmured regretfully, wishing she could stay longer.

"I still wish the team could be wearing their new name Sunday," he muttered, opening the door to the hall.

He turned back to Marty. "I'll be on that plane tomorrow," he said. "I happen to have the seat next to yours."

It was late when Marty finally tumbled into her own bed. After convincing Jerry that she could get another ride home so he and Pauline would have a little more time together, Marty then had to convince Rick that he couldn't leave his other guests. In the end, she rode home with Vicky.

The special glow in Rick's eyes when he'd bid her good night kept her awake for a couple of hours after she turned out the light. Even though she tried to tell herself that it was only excitement from the upcoming trip that made her restless, her heart knew better. It was the time she'd spent alone with Rick that made her toss and turn, not the worry that she might forget to pack her favorite mitt.

CHAPTER SIX

Rick had offered Marty a ride to the airport on Saturday morning, but her father was taking her. Mr. Gibson's gesture had been unexpected, but welcome. Now, as they walked into the terminal, Marty's larger suitcase in her father's grip, she was glad of his solid presence.

Even though Marty traveled frequently and had flown several times, excitement and nervousness were taking over. Her father checked her in, surrendered her bags, and stood by quietly as she greeted some of her teammates. Before she noticed he'd left, he was back with coffee in a styrofoam cup.

She sipped it gratefully, eyeing the others from the team. They stood in small groups with spouses and boyfriends, talking and laughing.

Her father saw the direction of her gaze. "I'll be getting along," he said. "I'm meeting Sam Marshall for nine holes."

Marty brought her attention back to Mr. Gibson. "I really appreciate the lift," she said, wanting to say more but not sure how.

"Do you have enough money?" His hand reached for his back pocket.

Marty stopped him with a touch on his arm. "I'm fine."

He frowned, thick gray eyebrows pulled together. "Well," he said, clearing his throat. "Good luck, and have a nice time."

Marty nodded, moisture filming her eyes momentarily.

"Take care," he added, patting her shoulder awkwardly.

"I will."

As he turned away, she said, "Dad." When he looked back, her arms went around his neck. She muttered, "Thanks," against his shirt. She felt his arms briefly enclose her before they both stepped back. He turned without comment and walked quickly away.

Marty smiled to herself, glad she had followed her impulse even if it had embarrassed him. Physical signs of affection were rare between them, but the hug felt right. Somehow Marty had sensed his caring this morning, even through his stern veneer.

She was still standing by Gate 4 when Rick spotted her. His pulse accelerated and a prickling sensation danced across his skin. He wondered at the tiny smile that curved her lips temptingly as she stared bemusedly past him.

As he strode closer, Marty's gaze shifted. There was welcome, and more, on her face. As she took a first step toward him, Vicky glanced over. In seconds Rick was surrounded.

"Where are the new uniforms?" one of the outfielders asked. "I thought you were bringing them."

99

"Didn't they come yet?" Ann, the second base-man, stomped her foot. "I was looking forward to new duds for the tourney."

Rick sought Marty's face in the group, feeling outnumbered. "They're lost," he explained to the knot of women surrounding him. "Penn Sport shipped them out and I never got them."

A chorus of groans met his announcement.

Marty pushed through the group. "I hope everyone brought her old uniform," she said. "We won a lot of games with them, and we can win a few more."

"I guess so," Vicky muttered. "My mom did tailor mine to my *personal* measurements." The way she pushed out her chest left no doubt about which measurement she meant.

"Thanks for trying, Rick," Pauline told him before drifting away with some of the others.

He and Marty exchanged a long look. "Thanks," he said softly. "For a moment I was afraid they were going to tie me to the wing."

They were seated on the 737 and the plane taxied to the runway, its jet engines beginning to roar. He took Marty's hand in his. Marty's fingers curled, lightly touching the calloused skin of his palm and her heart beat a little faster.

The takeoff was smooth, the flight uneventful. Even the transfer from one plane to another in Chicago was accomplished with a minimum of hassle. Marty hoped that their luggage and ball gear had made the transfer with the same degree of efficiency.

Hours later, as the 737 banked and went into its final approach, her gaze was glued to the window. The Cascade range broke free of the surrounding area with a kind of fierce arrogance, jutting toward heaven with primitive beauty. After crossing the mountains, they glided over countless acres of evergreen forest as smooth and even as grass. Lake Washington passed beneath them like a dark opal set into a surrounding panorama of emerald velvet.

Rick leaned toward her, pointing out Bellevue and Mercer Island as their altitude decreased. The aroma of his cologne mingling with his own personal scent distracted Marty from what he was telling her. With considerable effort, she concentrated on his words as he pointed out different landmarks during the descent to Seattle. Within moments the runway at Sea-Tac airport was rushing up to meet them.

After they deplaned, Marty found herself swept into a laughing group of ball players on their way to the baggage terminal. She knew that Rick's sister was going to meet him. Feeling strangely shy, Marty allowed herself to be carried along with the others. When she looked back, Rick was walking with a dark-haired woman, his gaze skimming the crowded concourse.

She saw him again at the baggage pickup, but pretended not to notice his raised hand as Pauline commandeered a taxi. Instinctively, Marty realized that she needed a breather. She ducked into the cab with Pauline and Betty.

Rick had explained that his sister and her husband were remodeling their house and didn't have room to put him up. Marty had mixed feelings about being in the same hotel with him.

One of the tire stores in Allentown had donated money for rental cars. After checking in, Vicky, Pauline, and Betty left with one of the tournament hosts to pick them up. Marty stayed in the room she was sharing with Pauline. There had been no opportunity to ask her about Jerry, but Marty could tell that the younger woman was happy just by looking at her beaming face.

Marty jumped when the phone in her room rang.

"What happened to you?" Rick demanded in response to her soft greeting. "I wanted you to meet Karen."

"I'm sorry," Marty replied. "I caught a ride over with some of the others." Even his familiar voice on the phone made her tense. Her free hand strayed to the back of her neck, where the muscles were beginning to knot.

"My sister would like you to come out for dinner," he said. "I can pick you up in an hour." His voice was commanding.

"I'm sorry," Marty said, rebelling. "I really wanted to rest tonight. I—"

A crisp expletive sizzled through the telephone wires. "You sound like an eighty-year-old spinster," Rick snapped. "You don't even play till Monday. The only thing going tomorrow is the opening ceremonies. How much rest do you need to stand in the sun for a half hour?"

Marty silently counted to ten. "I—"

Again he cut her off. "I'm sorry. Could we start over?" His voice had miraculously changed from raw whiskey to warm honey. It flowed over Marty like a sensual caress, making her wish he was in the room with her.

Somehow she forgot once again all her sensible resolutions. "I'd love to meet your sister." The words squeezed past the building emotion that threatened to choke her.

After unpacking and relaxing in a hot bath,

Marty was trying to decide between the aqua dress, which had traveled without wrinkling, and a print blouse and tailored slacks. A key scraped in the door. He wouldn't—

Pauline walked in, jangling her room key. "Hi, kid. How ya doing?" she asked, throwing herself on the other bed.

"Not so hot," Marty muttered absently. The clothes she'd brought seemed perfectly adequate until Rick's invitation. Now she was torn between too dressy and too casual.

"What's the problem?" Pauline asked curiously. "Did you pick up a guy already?"

Marty shook her head. "I'm going to dinner at Rick's sister's. What do you think?" She held up each outfit.

"The pants. Nobody in Seattle dresses up."

Pauline's words bounced back at Marty as she and Rick walked into the foyer of his sister's home. The brunette Marty had seen at the airport was wearing a ruffled sundress.

"I'm glad you could come," she said with an easy smile. "I've been wanting to meet you."

Rich flung a proprietary arm around Marty's shoulders. "Karen, this is the girl I told you so much about." His words spun Marty's heart around like a runaway Frisbee. He must be more serious about her than she'd imagined.

"She's the hottest female pitcher in Pennsylvania," he added, popping Marty's rosy bubble with one jab. "This is my only sister, Karen," he told her, unaware of the fantasy he'd created and destroyed in less than two heartbeats.

Within minutes Marty had met Bob, Karen's husband, and her two children, Jeremy and

Megan. Bob was wearing a barbecue apron and brandishing a long spatula.

"I'm doing some fresh trout on the grill," Bob explained, seeing Marty eye his apron. "Just caught them yesterday."

Megan looked about eight, the boy younger. He was a miniature of his uncle, right down to the navy-blue eyes. Marty felt a sharp pain in the general region of her heart.

Dinner was casual, fish, salad, and rice pilaf eaten amid much laughter and teasing between Rick and his sister. The kids contributed random comments about their summer and the coming school year. It was obvious that their Uncle Rick was a big favorite with them. Bob grumbled lightly about cutbacks at the shipyard where he was an engineer.

Both Bob and Karen asked Marty all about her job, obviously fascinated with her interest in the use of solar energy.

"For decades we've had cheap electric power in the Northwest," Bob told her. "But things are changing. People in this area are becoming very aware of alternate methods. We're adding extra insulation as we remodel the house."

"Perhaps you could give us some ideas before you leave town," Karen suggested.

During the drive back to the hotel, Rick glanced over at Marty, and an unaccustomed tenderness almost overwhelmed him. It temporarily pushed aside the raw desire that was his constant companion lately. She was in for a brutal few days, and he wondered how prepared she was emotionally for what she would be facing. He didn't always understand her, but had confidence that she would give the challenge everything she had.

She was very good at what she did, but so vulnerable in many ways. The protective instincts that welled up in him when he thought of her alone on the pitcher's mound were surprising. Usually those instincts were directed toward saving his own hide.

Marty's head was filled with fantasies about children of her own, with Rick as their father. The rented Ford sped through the dusk of the Seattle evening, and her hands curled into tight balls as she faced the truth. As unwise, foolish, impractical, and hopeless a situation as she knew it to be, she'd fallen head over heels in love with Rick Stokes.

The knowledge hit her like a huge fist, slamming the breath from her. When she'd finally begun to recover from the devastating shock, she sneaked a look at Rick. He glanced at her and smiled.

"Tired?" he inquired, turning down the radio.

Marty nodded, but felt disappointed that he didn't know what she was really feeling. Didn't she look different to him? Couldn't he see the sudden change?

Rick stopped at a red light and gazed at her again. She looked fragile in the glow from the streetlights. How he wished he could lend her his strength and experience, but he wasn't sure how she'd take advice from him. She must be nervous about the upcoming challenge. Her eyes were as big as coat buttons.

Then he remembered her poise when she'd faced him from the pitcher's mound and he knew without a doubt that she would be just fine. All there remained for him to do was to smooth the way and oversee the details.

And not add any extra pressures like taking her to bed. Sexual tension shuddered through him at the thought of how her soft skin would feel against his own. With a silent groan he gripped the steering wheel until he was afraid it would snap.

Marty saw him scowl at the green light before he eased the car through the intersection. What was wrong now, she wondered as she huddled closer to the passenger door.

They didn't exchange a word until Rick stopped at the door to Marty's room. She dug the key from her purse and he turned her silently toward him. It was more than Marty could do to look into his face. What she had just discovered was still too new and she was afraid he would see it and be dismayed by her unwanted love.

"Marty," he breathed softly, crooking one finger under her chin and tilting her face upward. His breath caught at her sheer loveliness as she finally met his gaze. The hallway light turned her eyes into mysterious pools. Sadness seemed to lurk there for an instant, banished then by a sweep of her thick lashes. Her skin was pale in the ghostly glow and as fine-textured as that of a baby, her mouth a glistening cushion to rest his hungry lips upon.

The hallway was deserted. Rick succumbed to the temptation of her beautiful lips and pulled her against him. Her mouth opened slightly beneath the crush of his and his tongue dove hotly, betraying his loss of control. One hand touched the curve of her breast through her thin blouse.

Marty arched helplessly, leaning into his caress. Rick's other hand traced her spine to the rounded curve below, pressing her against the heat of his arousal. He felt her response rocket through them

106

both, and for one wild moment he considered pulling her into his own room a few doors down.

His lips broke from hers and he dragged in a burning breath. The elevator pinged softly around the corner, signaling its arrival, and his grip relaxed further, as shreds of sanity began to struggle against the primitive emotions that gripped him. Much as he wanted to make her his, he couldn't complicate her life when it was already filled with so much.

Marty was nestled against him, panting softly, as they both listened to receding footsteps. Then Rick pulled her close again, pressing her cheek against his wildly racing heart. "I want you," he whispered. "But the timing is terrible. You need every bit of your concentration for the upcoming ordeal, and I wouldn't want to share you. It's better we say good night now."

Marty stiffened. His kiss had aroused her past any logical considerations, but apparently *he* could still think coolly. The knowledge was hurtful. She wanted him spinning out of control as she was, his only driving thought to be one with her. Instead, calm reason intruded upon what could have been a night of unforgettable loving.

Rick must have sensed something of her thoughts as he set her away and reached to take her key. His hand froze and his eyes narrowed. Their gazes locked. Marty watched, fascinated as his pupils expanded and a hot flush spread across his cheeks. The hand that had meant to take her key gripped her wrist instead, and she felt a tremor shake him.

"The hell with that," he grunted. "Nobility is a cold bedfellow and I've been without you far too long."

He raised her captive wrist to his burning

mouth and placed a kiss against her rampant pulse. Marty leaned against him weakly as his tongue touched her skin and her knees turned to Jell-O. He was all magnificent male, aroused and wanting. Flames of desire licked at Marty. She knew she would do anything he wanted. He was about to lead her down the hall when the door to her room opened.

"Ooh, bad timing." Pauline grinned at them impudently. "I thought you forgot your key," she explained to Marty.

After a moment of silence she shrugged and started to close the door. "Don't mind me," she said, and shut it firmly. "Carry on."

The interruption was enough to shatter the intimacy that had been building. Even the chance for one last kiss was lost as an older couple came out of the room opposite.

"I'll see you tomorrow," Rick said, frustration bracketing his passionate mouth with deep lines. "Would you ride to the field with me?"

Marty nodded, still shaky from their last embrace. "Thank you for tonight," she murmured, slipping into the room. She shut the door quickly, trying to adopt an indifferent attitude before facing Pauline.

The next day all the members of Bower of Flowers were dressed in their blue uniforms and waiting to be called onto the main field at Fort Dent, where the tournament would get underway after the opening ceremonies. Already the field was dense with ball players in a rainbow of different uniforms. Marty's group was the last of the eighteen participating teams to be introduced.

After every group had been presented and the

welcoming speeches delivered, the teams disbursed, scattering like brightly colored flowers in the wind. A flare gun signaled the start of the tournament, and four teams moved toward two adjacent fields for the first games. Marty's team wasn't scheduled to play until the next day.

Rick caught up to her amid the knowing glances of the others. Marty wondered what they all thought of her relationship with him. Heck, she didn't wonder, she knew. Most of them thought she was sleeping with him. She could tell by their envious looks.

Oblivious to the stares, Rick put his hand on her shoulder, turning her to face him. "How about doing some sight-seeing with me this afternoon?" he asked, looking devastating in his cerulean-blue knit shirt and tight jeans. Marty's gaze wandered down his powerful tanned arm before working its way back up to his broad chest, in silent appreciation of his raw male strength.

Misinterpreting her lack of verbal response, he added, "I'm an experienced guide. I've done Seattle several times with Megan and Jeremy, and I know all the best spots."

"Best spots for what?" she baited.

"Best spots to get lost," he said with a chuckle.

"Sounds like an offer I shouldn't refuse," Marty responded. "But first I had better change into something less conspicuous."

After lunch they took a tour of Underground Seattle, dropping behind the tour group so often that the guide became exasperated. Rick finally slipped him a tip to let them get lost.

Marty sauntered with Rick through the man-made caverns beneath Seattle's sidewalks, exchanging teasing kisses and burning glances. If his large hand wasn't gripping hers tightly, fingers entwined, his muscular arm was draped possessively across her shoulders. After a while Marty's lips became swollen from his insistent kisses, and her cheeks were flushed with the same joyful emotion that turned her gray eyes to molten pewter.

The next stop was Seattle's famous public market. Rick and Marty wandered its length, stopping at artfully arranged displays of mammoth crabs and salmon, ducking into tiny shops that sold everything from handmade jewelry to specially blended herb teas.

At one jewelry stall Rick picked out a dolphin on a chain fashioned from mother-of-pearl and silver. Overriding Marty's protests, he purchased it and fastened the delicate chain around her neck. The dolphin fell into the vee between the tops of her breasts. Rick stared for a moment at the pendant winking from the opening of her plaid blouse.

"That's where my mouth belongs," he whispered into her ear, pulling her close. "Loving every sweet, curving inch of you."

His words made her tremble with longing.

Moments later they were seated in a small booth in a tiny Mexican restaurant across from the market. Hot food and cold beer quelled one of Marty's hungers while the other raged. Rick's smile over his plate of rice and enchiladas was relaxed and friendly, as if he'd already forgotten the words that had seared Marty's ears.

After the spicy meal Rick lifted Marty's hand to his mouth. One by one, he took her sticky fingers between his lips and bathed them with his tongue. His gaze never wavered as he finally pressed his open mouth against her palm, then curled her fingers around the kiss he'd left there.

He slid from the booth and, feeling thoroughly ravaged, Marty managed to support herself on shaking legs as he tugged her to her feet. She followed him silently, her brain too agitated to form even the simplest words, never mind whole sentences.

On the way back to the car they stopped to listen to the frenzied fiddling of a street musician, Rick's arm holding Marty close. As they moved on, he dropped a folded bill into the battered hat on the cement at the fiddler's feet.

"Thank you, kind sir," the long-haired musician called out, his fingers and bow flying over his instrument.

At an outdoor flower stall Rick insisted on picking out a huge orange chrysanthemum for Marty's hair.

"Pin it on the side that shows you're spoken for," he told her, voice husky with desire.

Marty congratulated herself for her outward calm as she asked, "Which side is that? I flunked Polynesian Folklore 101."

Before starting the car, Rick took Marty's hand and placed it on his thigh. During the trip back to the hotel she was acutely aware of every ripple of his powerful muscles each time he braked or accelerated. It seemed that her heart braked and her pulses accelerated with the vehicle each time his warm flesh shifted under her hand.

Rick's actions throughout the afternoon both elated and confused her. Each move, each look, each kiss had stamped her as his. His gaze burned with passion, his hands were hot with it. More than once a muscle jerked in his cheek when she returned his sizzling glances, her eyes soft and dreamy, her lips moist from his kisses. Marty knew where it was all leading and she gloried in the knowledge.

Pulling into a slot in the hotel's parking garage, Rick leaned across the seat and branded her mouth once again with a searing kiss. A tiny moan bubbled up from Marty's throat and he drank the sound with greed, his tongue probing deeper at her passionate response.

"It wasn't my intention to take you in the car," he murmured, pulling back. "But, by God, that's what I'll do if we stay here much longer."

Marty showed no reluctance at his blunt declaration. Her eyes met and held Rick's smoldering stare. A tremor shook his taut body as he reached for the car door.

The trip through the lobby was accomplished without delay. An empty elevator stood open. Rick moved forward swiftly as its doors began to glide shut, pulling Marty in behind him. The ride to the fourth floor was spent sharing a kiss that consumed Marty's soul. Her heart went up in flames. Unspoken messages crackled between them as they walked hand in hand to Rick's room.

Entering ahead of him, Marty looked around nervously.

"Why don't you sit down?" Rick suggested gently. He could tell that Marty had grown tense, so he tried to put her at ease. "Would you like something to drink? Some wine?"

Marty bobbed her head. Her complexion had paled and her expression was closed and he had no idea what she was thinking. She intrigued him as no other woman ever , had. Returning the unopened wine bottle to the cabinet, he held out his hand.

"Come here," he said quietly. Marty didn't move. "Come and warm me, love." For a timeless moment the only sounds in the room were shallow breathing and the subdued traffic noises from below. As Marty stared at the broad hand extended to her, it quivered. His strengths had attracted her; his exposed need was her undoing.

Her own hunger was etched across her face as she rose and stepped into arms that closed around her trembling body. Marty clung to Rick, letting the mingled aromas of his warm body fill her senses. Never had she been so certain of anything as she was of the commitment she was about to make.

Marty was sure that Rick's feelings didn't match her own. He wanted her, he'd made that very clear. For now it was enough. Perhaps that was all there would ever be between them, but Marty was too filled with desire for this special man to care.

His hands slid lightly down her spine to press into the deep indentation of her waist. His mouth covered hers. There was no hesitation in the kiss, only need too long denied. Passion held in check now flowed like a river in flood. The touch of Rick's hot mouth fueled an answering lust in Marty and she opened beneath the sensual onslaught. Her fingers tangled in his hair, holding his head, while she met his insistence with demands of her own.

Their tongues teased and stroked while he pressed her tighter. Rick's physical response, impossible to hide, surged against the cradle of Marty's hips. When she arched her neck to give his

113

marauding lips better access to the sensitive skin of her throat, her lower body nestled closer to the thrust of his desire.

A soft groan was torn from Rick's throat. One large hand slid down the length of delicate chain until his questing fingers found the top button of her blouse, right below the silver dolphin. His mouth followed his fingers, bestowing searing kisses on the soft flesh that swelled above her bra.

Marty's own hands sought the feel of Rick's bare skin, skimming lightly from the nape of his neck to settle boldly on the fastenings of his shirt. Inserting two fingers into the opening between the buttons, she lightly scored her nails across his chest.

A tremor shook him as he lifted his mouth from its devotion to her breasts, still confined by sheerest lace. His dark blue eyes blazed into hers, the intense light from them almost blinding in its clarity.

"Sweetheart, you make me crazy with hunger for you," he breathed, his arms forming a sweetly erotic cage around her. "Let me love you. I've waited so long."

Marty, too, had unconsciously been waiting for someone like Rick. No, for Rick alone to set fire to her senses, to awaken her woman's body as no one else had ever done. Wild to show him how much she loved him, even if she couldn't yet speak the words, she pulled his head down and pressed her willing mouth to his in an answer impossible to misinterpret.

Rick took her in his arms and lifted her. For a moment the room spun crazily. Then he nestled her against the rapid pounding of his heart and carried her to the bed.

Marty gazed at him with the most trusting expression. He felt a tightening in his throat as he tendered his precious burden. Studying her wide-set silver eyes, the slim bridge of her nose ending in a pert tip dotted with freckles, and finally the sweet curve of her mouth, his arms tightened a fraction before he leaned forward, setting her on the bed.

"You don't know how many times I dreamed of being with you like this," he murmured tenderly as she clung to him.

"I felt the same way," she gasped. He bent and kissed her upturned nose before resting his lips against hers in a kiss filled with promise.

Marty's arms fell away and he straightened, his piercing gaze never leaving hers as he undid the buttons her hungry fingers had missed. Pulling the shirt away, he tossed it aside and joined her on the bed.

Marty's clothing seemed to melt from her overheated body, replaced by Rick's skillful hands and loving mouth. Every inch of her longed to feel his imprint. Her arms held him, her nails scoring his flesh lightly until she forgot everything but feeling and need.

Even as she urged him closer, driven wild with hunger, he paused to kiss her tenderly. Raising up, he swiftly shed the remainder of his clothing. "Not yet," he murmured as Marty's eager arms embraced him.

She writhed beneath him, her seeking hands flowing over the muscles of his back, moving around to tangle in the soft hair that arrowed from his broad chest downward. As she followed its path, Rick quivered.

A hard knee parted Marty's thighs and Rick's

fingers found and gently explored her. At his intimate touch, she arched and opened to him.

"Please," she moaned. "Come to me."

The words inflamed him. His hands cupped her hips and he shifted forward. Slowly he entered her. Sheathed within the satiny warmth, he felt his tightly held control fragment. Sweat dampened his heated skin as he started to thrust.

The gentle vise that held Rick began a sweet spasm around him. At Marty's cry of surprise and fulfillment, his control shattered completely and he plunged one last time, burying himself deep within her. He called out Marty's name as he exploded in ecstasy.

CHAPTER SEVEN

The clock beside Rick's bed showed nine P.M. when Marty awoke. The room was dark and she snuggled against his warm body, feeling replete and happy.

"Hi." Rick's voice was deep and soft. His hand smoothed back Marty's tangled hair before he raised up on one elbow. Even though she couldn't make out his expression in the room's darkness, Marty felt a deep intimacy, certain they had shared much more than merely a physical joining.

Her hand rested on the flat muscles of his chest, the downy hair tickling her palm, as she echoed his greeting.

"Watch your eyes," he cautioned, reaching for the light.

Marty was tempted to burrow beneath the covers. Instead she bravely faced him in the glow of the lamp, knowing that her hair was a mess and her makeup had long since been kissed away.

"Our morning after came a little early," she tried to joke.

Tiny lines around his eyes crinkled as he smiled

down at her. "I'd love to keep you here till morning. But we don't want to worry your roommate."

Marty sprang up to a sitting position, forgetting her nudity until the sheet fell away. Too late she grabbed for it as Rick's eyes widened with interest.

"On second thought . . ." His voice trailed off as he pressed her onto the mattress. "You could get back from dinner at ten as easily as at nine. Tell her we stayed for dessert."

Marty's giggles filled the silence, to be abruptly cut off by his marauding lips.

It was slightly after ten when she slipped on her shoes and tried to tame her hair with Rick's comb. Looking at her reflection in the mirror, she thought that what she'd been doing would be obvious to anyone. Stepping from the bathroom, she glanced at the man who stood looking out the window. He turned and walked quickly to her side.

"I have something for you," he said, placing a chaste kiss on her forehead. "It's for the game tomorrow."

Marty's forehead wrinkled with puzzlement as he opened a dresser drawer and pulled out something long and white. His expression was slightly sheepish as he held out the tattered item.

"Perhaps you think it's silly," he said. "But I want you to have my lucky socks."

During warm-ups before the first game, against a team from Alaska, Marty was having an awful time concentrating. Reminders of the night before kept intruding, Rick's ardor and his patience, her own passionate response. Marty flushed hotly as she recalled the touch of his skilled hands and lips on her most sensitive places. Her heart felt

118

ready to burst with happiness. Dropping the ball into her mitt, she brushed one finger against her mouth, remembering with a sense of wonder how it had flowered under his.

A shout from the umpire shattered the rosy memory. Marty blinked slowly, then focused on home plate as her ingrained professionalism took over. With great effort she banished all thoughts of Rick and their evening together as the first batter stepped into the box.

The other team tried hard, but they were no match for Marty's pitching and her teammates' hot bats and impenetrable defense. Bower of Flowers ended up beating Fairbanks Charters 15–3.

Their good luck held for most of the week. When they weren't playing, Marty was seeing as much of the city as possible with Rick, visiting with his sister and her family, or sharing his bed.

On Wednesday there was no game. Rick and Marty took a picnic lunch to his sister's cabin on the Skykomish River, above a small town named Index. After walking along the river, skipping rocks and dunking bare toes into the icy mountain water, they made love beneath a majestic stand of Douglas firs. Every night Marty slept in the room she shared with Pauline; every day she and Rick grew closer.

The team's luck changed Saturday evening when they lost to a scrappy hometown team before a grandstand full of local fans. A walk and two errors made the final score 2–1 in favor of Seattle. On Sunday morning the Bower rallied to beat a tough team from Texas in five extra innings, winning the right to face one of the top women's teams, the Golden Angels from Los Angeles. The

119

Angels had just returned from a tour of New Zealand and were expected to win the tournament. Marty had heard that their budget was five times that of her team. There was a tendency to believe the rumor when they drove onto the field in five gold Cadillacs.

"I wish I'd thought of that," Rick was heard to mutter from the Bower's dugout.

In the first game of their doubleheader with the Angels, Pat started the substitute pitcher they'd picked up after the regional tournament to replace Louise. Tournament rules stated that Bower of Flowers had to defeat the unbeaten California team twice to win the national title. The pitcher got into trouble in the second inning, loading the bases and forcing Pat to put in Marty. Normally she would have saved her best pitcher for the championship game.

Marty managed to win the first game, but exhaustion from the earlier, extra-inning game against Texas proved too great a handicap during the second. The Angels carried four pitchers on their roster, but Bower of Flowers had only two. Despite their best efforts, Marty's team could only finish the tournament in second place.

Rick sat down next to her in the dugout as Marty changed her shoes. "Tough way to lose," he commented gruffly. "How are you doing?"

"I'm okay." As she said the words, Marty realized it was true. She was disappointed, but not crushed. Given different circumstances, her team might have won. But they did finish second and that was no small potatoes. They had done well in front of all those fans, and had every right to be proud.

Marty slipped into her blue team jacket and

Rick picked up her equipment bag. For once she was proud of his possessiveness. The season was over and her relationship with Rick now belonged only to the two of them. There was no longer any need to worry about it disrupting team harmony or causing other problems.

At the end of a meeting held on the grassy sidelines, there was much mumbling and giggling. Marty and Rick stood off to one side. Everyone else seemed to have the same attitude as Marty. There was disappointment, but also a deep pride in their season record.

Marty looked up to see the rest of the team approaching. Pauline cleared her throat.

"We all think you deserve the game ball," she told Marty. "Everyone signed it."

Sudden tears welled up in Marty's eyes as she took the ball from Pauline. After juggling it in her hand for a moment, she turned to Rick and pulled a pen from his shirt pocket.

"I really appreciate this," she told the others, carefully writing her name on a bare spot. "It's a great honor and I don't take it lightly. But I think you'll all agree that there's one person who really made possible our being here."

She stopped and took a deep breath, wiping at her eyes. The gesture left a streak of dust across her cheek. "There's someone else here who had faith in us, who's only been part of our team for a short time."

Turning to a surprised Rick, she held out the ball. "Without your support, we wouldn't be here," she said, thrusting it into his hands. "Thank you, and thanks for the socks," she added, patting her back pocket. I'm sure they helped get us into second place."

"Socks?" Vicky echoed. "I didn't get any socks."

Rick was startled by Marty's gesture, but his hand closed around the ball automatically. The women on the team cheered wildly, some yelling, "Speech, speech!"

He found that he was more moved than he had been in a very long time. It was difficult to talk past the lump of pride and emotion that had formed in his throat, but he managed to get out a few words about how pleased he was before he was mobbed.

Marty stood to one side, a silly grin on her face, while the others hugged and kissed him. Rick was overwhelmed to feel so much a part of a group he'd first looked down on with superior male scorn.

The first person Marty saw when she walked into the airport terminal was her father. When she'd told him on the telephone of their final loss and the time of her flight back, he hadn't said much. She'd expected him to comment on her earlier cockiness, but he'd only asked how she was.

Now Marty walked toward him, wishing she had a championship trophy in her hand, instead of the team cup for second place. She saw Jerry rush past, but he had eyes only for Pauline and didn't even notice Marty.

As Mr. Gibson waited for her, his face seemed softer than usual, his bearing less rigid. There was unaccustomed hesitation in his manner as he stood there.

"I'm sorry, honey," he said when she stopped before him. "I know the title would've meant a lot to you. But that's a beautiful trophy."

It was the first time he'd acknowledged how

important softball was to Marty, and his admission surprised her.

He slid an arm around her shoulders, which surprised her even more. "I'm damned proud of you," he said gruffly.

Rick's steps had slowed, giving Marty a few minutes with her father. As he walked up to greet the gray-haired man, he glanced at the young woman who had become so important to him. Her silver eyes were swimming with unshed tears. Knowing that she would be embarrassed at the temporary loss of composure, he turned to her father.

"They did great, sir. Marty pitched fantastic ball."

"I wish I could have been there," Mr. Gibson answered. "I should have gone."

Marty's mouth fell open, making such a comic picture that it was all Rick could do not to throw back his head and laugh. He disguised a chuckle by turning it into a cough before making his excuses and a discreet exit so that Marty could ride home with her father.

The next morning she was plowing through the mountain of papers that had accumulated on her desk while she'd been gone, still seething over the remark her father had made in the car the day before. He'd commented that the near win in Seattle was a fitting end to Marty's career. Then he'd reminded her that it was time to turn her attention to finding a man and starting a family. Just when she'd begun to feel he understood her a little.

She slammed shut a desk drawer and dropped a folder on the desk. Then the door to Gibson Enterprises burst open. A wide smile flashed across her face as she looked up to see Rick standing before her. The three-piece charcoal gray suit he wore with a white shirt and crimson silk tie was a perfect complement to his athletic body and tanned face. Marty never tired of looking at him, in jeans or dressed to kill as he was now. The rhythm of her heart accelerated, and she felt warmer. Feeling almost painfully vulnerable to the man who stood before her, she attempted a light greeting meant to disguise her strong reaction to his presence.

"Break a window, Mr. Stokes?" she asked in a teasing voice.

"I would if I had to," he said, before glancing around the deserted office. Sitting on the corner of her desk, he leaned over and placed a swift, hard kiss on her upturned mouth.

"I missed you last night."

His possessive words made her pulse, already pounding rapidly, do a happy little dance within her. "I missed you too, but I had so much to do before work today. Even though Dad told me not to come in, I needed to get back."

He nodded. "I understand, sweetie, but I was still lonesome."

As her bemused brain tried to form a reply, he spoke again. "I'm here with an invitation."

Before he could elaborate, Mr. Gibson walked in. After greeting the older man, Rick turned back to Marty. "I have a convention in Reno next week. I know that you've missed a lot of work, but I'm hoping you can get the time off to go with me. Have you ever been there?"

Marty shook her head. Another week with Rick! It sounded like heaven. As quickly as her spirits had soared, they plummeted. She couldn't ask for more time off, and she told Rick that. Then, before she could prevent him, he addressed her father.

Marty's temper began to heat up. The two men discussed the trip as if she wasn't even present. Rick explained when they had to leave and how long they'd be gone.

Her father scratched his chin. "Jerry's friend, Bob, has been doing a great job filling in for Martha," he said, mulling over the idea.

Marty rose from her chair, intending to break into their discussion. Her father's next words stopped her cold.

"A lot of couples take advantage of Reno's relaxed regulations while they're in town," he hinted, smiling. "Perhaps your tour of the city will include one of those twenty-four-hour wedding chapels."

Marty's eyes bugged out at his heavy-handed suggestion. Next he'd be offering Rick ten chickens and a pig to take her off his hands! No wonder he wasn't upset with the idea of his only daughter going off for a week with the likes of Rick Stokes! He viewed the younger man as a prospective son-in-law.

"Dad!" she exclaimed, furious. "It's a vacation, not a honeymoon." Highly embarrassed, she turned to Rick for support. He was silent, his expression impossible to read. Confused, she also became speechless, the words that had been ready to erupt fizzling away like flat champagne.

"You can have the time off," her father said.

"Do you want to go?" Rick asked at the same time.

"Yes," Marty snapped. "And thank you," she told her father crossly. Men!

125

The evening before they were to leave for Reno, Marty was preparing dinner for Rick at her apartment. The subject of their possible elopement hadn't come up again with either Rick or her father, and Marty had done her best to forget the whole embarrassing incident.

Cornish hens were baking in the oven and a garden salad chilled in the fridge. Her kitchen was modern but compact and convenient. The floor and tiled counters were almond beige, and Marty had added frilly curtains in a cream, rust, and royal-blue Pennsylvania Dutch print.

From the kitchen she walked into the living room. Biscuit-colored carpeting spread beneath a rust-and-tan plaid sectional. Bookshelves covered one wall and a stereo was positioned next to a bar on the other wall.

Sliding doors behind tweedy-tan draperies led to a postage-stamp–sized balcony. Empty corners in the comfortable living room were disguised with leafy green plants. Marty had begun most of them from tiny starts acquired from friends.

Satisfied that everything looked neat and clean, she went back into the kitchen to check the birds' progress. They were browning nicely and she basted them before closing the oven door. When the telephone rang, she hoped that nothing had happened to delay Rick. Dinner was right on schedule and she already missed him terribly.

After a brief conversation, Marty poured herself a glass of wine and plopped down on the couch, despite the fact that she was still wearing her robe and a bare face. She was in shock, but a few sips of wine helped to calm her.

After several minutes she let out an unfeminine

whoop of pure pleasure and danced into the bedroom to dress for Rick's arrival. She could hardly wait to share her news.

"You're going where?" Rick asked, tasting the wine Marty had thrust into his hand before making her startling announcement. He couldn't believe that she was so excited about being away from him for a whole month. He was still trying to cope with the delectable sight of her in tight white jeans and a baby-pink knit top that clung to her sexy curves like a jealous lover. It was difficult, under the circumstances, to concentrate on what she was saying.

"California and Texas," she repeated. "They're forming an all-star team from the national tournament and I've been invited to be on it. We're touring both states. Isn't it exciting?" Marty's eyes sparkled.

"Uh, yeah." Rick didn't want to dampen her enthusiasm, but a *whole month*. Would her father give her that much more time off? Selfishly he hoped the answer would be no. He found it hard even to think about being separated from her that length of time. Well, perhaps he could join her on the road for a few days.

"I'm glad this is the last of it though," he added, taking another sip of his sparkling wine. "I'll miss you, babe."

"Last of what?" Marty's eyes clouded with confusion. Surely Rick didn't share her father's opinion that she should retire. She'd been thinking along those lines herself lately, but resented his inference that it was all settled.

Rick's dark eyes became opaque and his face impassive, as if he sensed he'd bungled. "From some of the things you said, I assumed you were thinking about quitting. You've been at the game a long time." His tone was cautious.

"And how long did you play?" she snapped.

"That was different. It was my career and I was getting paid for it."

"Oh, spare me that!" Marty set down the fragile wineglass with an unfragile thump that sloshed the clear liquid over the rim. "You sound just like my father." Her voice had gone up an octave and she determinedly lowered it. "I wish you'd both stay out of it."

Rick crossed the living room and attempted to put his arms around her. Marty jerked away, lower lip jutting petulantly. After taking a deep breath, Rick put a hand on her shoulder and turned her back around.

"I think it's terrific that you made the team," he said, voice much quieter than a few moments before. "I'll miss you, but I'll survive, and you'll have a great time." Marty relaxed against him. "Let's leave it at that for tonight, okay?" he asked.

She nodded as he held her close. "Okay."

After dinner Rick insisted on helping with the cleanup, which cancelled Marty's impression that he would be a dyed-in-the-wool chauvinist when it came to chores. She might love him, but was still dead wrong about him in some ways, she realized.

Nothing more had been said about her softball career, even though they'd discussed some of the places Marty would be visiting on her all-star tour. Rick had been to Sacramento, Houston, and several other larger cities she mentioned. She hadn't realized that he'd played A ball for two years in Arizona before the majors called him up. There were a lot of things about Rick she didn't know.

Marty was making coffee when he came up behind her and blew softly into her ear. She shivered in reaction.

"It's not coffee I need to warm me, woman. Why don't you leave that and we'll have it for breakfast."

Marty turned with a smile. "Don't you have to pack? The flight to Reno leaves at nine A.M." Her own luggage was ready to go, except for a couple of last-minute items.

"My bags are in the car. I'm all yours till flight time." His mouth smiled, but his eyes were serious. And hungry.

"I see you've got a timer for the coffee maker. Why don't you set it while I go to the car and grab my overnight case?" His expression was full of messages that could melt a girl's back fillings.

"Pretty sure of yourself, aren't you?" she teased.

In response Rick's mouth covered hers in a kiss so achingly sensual that Marty's hand gripped the counter behind her for support.

"Get your bag," she gasped when she could breathe again. "Don't dawdle either, mister."

When he returned, locking the outside door behind him, Marty melted against his big body, her arms sliding around his neck. Her soft curves fused with his hard male angles and she heard a sharp intake of breath. His response was immediate, and powerfully male.

Rick seared her mouth with a demanding kiss and caressed her breasts before scooping her into his muscular arms. He crossed the living room in long strides.

"The lights!" Marty exclaimed as they turned down the short hallway.

"Later," Rick growled. He kicked the bedroom

129

door shut behind them. "Much, much later," he murmured, allowing Marty to slide down his body like melting ice cream. "We're going to be very busy."

He sat on the edge of her double bed, removing his shoes, then lay back on the green-checkered gingham spread. "Come here, woman," he invited in velvety tones.

Kicking off her flats, Marty followed him. She sprawled across his taut body, rubbing against him and nuzzling his neck.

After a few moments of her seemingly naive wiggling, Rick rolled her onto her back, looming over her. "Much more of that," he rasped, "and we'll go to the main course and skip the appetizer altogether."

Marty batted her eyelashes at him in the dim light from the window. "Did I do something I shouldn't have?" she asked, eyes round with innocence, mouth pursed with suppressed laughter.

At the stark hunger etched on his face, her expression became serious. He stared at her mouth, his eyes emitting laser beams of passion. "You do everything you should," he whispered. "And so much more."

His open mouth burned against Marty's throat and a tiny cry escaped her lips. Her fingers tangled in his dark hair as she urged his marauding mouth to hers. With a fiery thrust his tongue plunged deep as one splayed hand slipped beneath her.

His hard male power burned against her softness as he pressed her closer. The shudder that ripped through him made her insides melt and flow in reaction. One of her long legs wrapped around his as she strained even closer. Rick lifted up to tug at her knit top. When he'd pulled it over

130

her head he imprisoned her wrists in its folds and held them lightly.

"You're so beautiful," he muttered hoarsely, staring down at her, braless and unadorned except for the silver dolphin on its chain.

Marty moaned with passion as hot male lips and driving tongue tormented the soft flesh and hardened tips of her high breasts. The gentle bite of his teeth on one sensitized bud made her arch upward, driving herself into his throbbing maleness.

With a final jerk he pulled the top from Marty's arms, releasing them. Her hands slid across the taut material of Rick's shirt, caressing his shoulders and back and then drifting to his waist. She tugged at handfuls of fabric, then burrowed under the loosened garment to explore his smooth skin.

Rick allowed her to push him over onto his back. Marty released each shirt button slowly, following with a lingering caress of the newly exposed skin. When she'd opened his shirt completely she rested against him, reveling in the tactile sensation of her soft breasts on the silky hair that covered his chest. Testing further, she moved lightly up and down.

The maneuver brought an immediate reaction from Rick, who had been doing his best to remain impassive while Marty played. He quickly stripped her and then himself of all remaining garments. His hands swept the length of her, followed closely by his hungry mouth.

Marty's gasps and responsive moans made the corners of his hard mouth turn upward as he searched out her most sensitive pleasure points. He missed nothing, from the hollow above her collarbone to the backs of her knees.

As his lips glided across the sweet curve of her

abdomen and his fingers parted the dark gold strands of silk below, her moans gave way to a sharp intake of breath. Rick's tongue caressed her hotly, insistently, and with each bold stroke her body arched higher. Her fingers clutched the bedspread material as she opened to him. With a final cry of passion, she exploded around his intimate kiss.

As her shudders of pleasure became slower, gentler, he slid up her body, seeking her mouth with his. Her trembling legs embraced his hips as he thrust deeply into her moist, still-quivering flesh. Rick's head was thrown back, his eyes tightly closed as his rhythm accelerated. Marty's legs locked firmly around him and a groan was wrenched from deep within him. One last driving stroke and his body lay fully upon her.

Ripples of pleasure still flowed through Marty as Rick's breathing steadied and deepened. The intensity of his loving had been more beautiful than anything she had ever experienced. Even as her hand shifted to stroke his hair, Rick spoke.

"I'm sorry," he whispered in the darkness. "You were so wonderful, so open and giving, you destroyed my control."

"Sorry? I don't understand."

"You will," he said as he began again to move within her.

Marty's body, replete only seconds before, responded quickly. "How . . . ?" she asked.

"I'm not a balloon," he answered, a tatter of laughter in his voice. "I don't collapse that quickly."

The climax that ripped through Marty's body prevented her from answering, perhaps even from hearing his explanation. She cried his name in helpless abandon, her curved fingers leaving half-moon indentations in his back.

Shifting his weight to the side, Rick gathered her precious body close as sleep claimed them both.

Sometime later Marty awoke to butterfly kisses whispering against her closed eyelids. Rick's hands began doing arousing, delicious things to her body as soon as he realized she was awake.

A sensual moan left her lips as they sought his. More quickly than she would have thought possible, she was writhing beneath him, wildly seeking the fulfillment only he could give her. As Marty plunged over the edge of the world, she felt Rick's final thrust, filling her with his life's essence.

As they came slowly back to earth, the shrill ring of the bedside phone slashed across the tiny bit of heaven they'd created in Marty's bedroom. When she glanced groggily at her clock radio, the luminous numbers showed her that it was only a little after one. Rick shifted beside her as she reached for the phone.

As he got to a sitting position, a warm hand cradling one naked breast, she reached to turn on the night-light.

"Hello," she managed in what she hoped was a normal tone.

During the brief, tense exchange she was dimly aware of Rick moving closer, his arm supporting and protecting her as he heard her sharp questions.

With a shaking hand, Marty replaced the receiver.

"That was Vera Flowers," she told Rick with tears in her voice. "She called from the hospital. Dad was having dinner at her place and she thinks he had a heart attack."

CHAPTER EIGHT

Rick slid out of bed and began pulling on his clothes. "Come on," he said. "I'll drive you to the hospital."

Marty stared at the clock radio on the nightstand. "You don't have to," she murmured, feeling numb. "It's one o'clock in the morning."

Shirt hanging open above the dark slacks he'd just zipped on, Rick circled to her side of the bed. When he took Marty's hand, her fingers curled tightly around his and she began to tremble.

"Don't be ridiculous," he said in a gentle voice. "I'm just glad I was here. Don't you realize how much I care about what happens to you?"

Marty looked up at him, a tiny frown puckering the skin between her fair brows. "Thank you." She couldn't seem to think straight, and waited for Rick to tell her what to do.

"Get dressed while I call the hospital and see if I can get some information." Gathering up his shoes and socks, Rick walked from the bedroom, shutting the door behind him. Marty scrambled up and began to dress as quickly as possible. After running

135

a comb through her hair, she entered the living room. Rick was replacing the telephone receiver.

"They've still got him in the emergency room, but he's stable," he said. "Are you ready to go?"

"I'm ready," she said in a small voice.

On the way to the hospital she belatedly remembered Rick's trip. "What about your flight?" she asked, torn between selfishness and self-sacrifice. "You don't want to miss the plane."

He glanced at her before returning his attention to the road he was speeding down as fast as he dared. "I'm not going. You don't really think I could dump you at the hospital and then leave town, do you?" His hand reached out to give hers a reassuring pat, then returned to the wheel. "I want to be here for you," he said, voice deep. "Is that okay?"

Marty sighed, feeling a slight lessening of the tension that had begun to replace the numbness. "That would be wonderful," she admitted.

When Marty and Rick rushed into the emergency room, Vera was sitting stiffly in a vinyl chair. She rose to her feet as they approached her.

"Thank goodness you're here," she said to Marty, nodding at Rick. "The specialist is with him now," she added, hugging Marty. "They're doing an EKG."

Dimly it registered that Vera was dressed in a very attractive slacks outfit. Her hair was tinted a becoming light brown. Marty was barely conscious of her own appearance in the first clothes she'd been able to grab, her hair sticking out in untidy spikes after a quick brushing. Her hands twisted together anxiously as a doctor came through the door.

"Are you Mr. Gibson's daughter?" he asked.

When she nodded, he continued briskly but not unkindly. "We won't be positive until we do more tests, but it looks like your father suffered an angina attack. Painful but not nearly as serious as a coronary. He's resting comfortably now, and I'd say he's out of any immediate danger."

"Can I see him?" Marty asked. A desperate need for reassurance gripped her. Rick's arm curved around her shoulders protectively.

"You can go in for five minutes," he told her. "But don't disturb him. He needs rest."

Vera hovered at Marty's elbow. The doctor turned his attention to her. "I suggest you come back in the morning, after ten," he said. "Mr. Gibson will be in his room and able to see you then."

Marty reached for Vera's hand. "Thanks for getting him here," she said to the older woman, noticing the worry lines on her round face. "And for calling me so quickly."

Vera nodded. "I should have called you right after the ambulance. I was just so shook up, and trying to keep Gordon still—"

"I understand," Marty said, a hundred questions about Vera's friendship with her father clamoring to be voiced. But Marty walked through the door to her father's room instead.

"Can we stay?" Rick asked Dr. Phillips before the other man had a chance to walk away.

He considered for a moment. "It would be better if you took Miss Gibson home," he said. "After he's settled in coronary care, he'll sleep the rest of the night. Tomorrow will be a long day for her, and she'll need some rest. We'll be monitoring Mr. Gibson closely."

* * *

It was late the next morning when Rick finally persuaded Marty to take a break and have a cup of coffee in the cafeteria. She nibbled at the toast he insisted on getting for her, then pushed away the heavy white plate.

Vera was upstairs with Mr. Gibson, and Rick sensed that she would appreciate a few more moments alone with him. She and Marty had alternated going into his room, only five minutes each hour. Other than the pasty color of his face, Mr. Gibson had looked reasonably well to Rick the one time he'd poked his head in to say hello.

The nurse had promised to page them in the cafeteria as soon as the doctor saw the results of the blood work.

Rick examined the dark smudges under Marty's eyes. He'd insisted she return to bed when they reached her apartment, and had slid in beside her to hold her close. She hadn't slept and neither had he. Finally, at about five, they'd showered and faced each other across her kitchen table while their coffee cooled in front of them.

After a few probing questions from him, she began to talk about growing up with her father after her mother's death. Rick could sense a deep affection between the two, despite Marty's statement that they had never been close. It seemed to Rick that they just hadn't communicated very well. He knew Mr. Gibson to be a quiet, rather stern man, but had seen evidence of pride and love in his eyes. Perhaps this scare would give them both the incentive to show their feelings more.

Now Dr. Phillips pulled out a chair and sat down next to Marty, a cup of black coffee in his hand. "I keep hoping they'll improve this stuff," he said, rubbing his eyes with bony fingers. "And they keep disappointing me."

Marty felt her face stiffen as she waited impatiently for him to get to the point. Without thinking, she reached for Rick's hand.

"We were right," the doctor said after taking a sip of the muddy brew. "It was an angina attack. If he feels like it, he can go home tomorrow. Mrs. Flowers has offered to look in on him, if that's okay. I spoke to her upstairs and she said she would be calling you."

Attempting to absorb the apparent seriousness of her father's relationship with Vera was too much for Marty as she also tried to adjust to the news that he hadn't suffered a heart attack. She pushed it aside for the time being. "Will his activities be limited?" she asked. "Will he have to be careful?"

Dr. Phillips shook his head. "I'll give you a booklet to read," he said. "But basically this was just a warning. Within reason, your father will be fine. He'll have to take medication, watch his diet, and exercise regularly. I've already discussed a little of that with him."

"What about work?" Marty asked. "It will be hard to keep him away for very long."

"He can go back in a week, if he feels up to it. I asked him about his job. Just make sure he doesn't lift anything heavy or get overly stressed. He'll be coming to see me before he goes back to work. Then we'll discuss golf and the other *important* things. I've already talked to him about walking every day, and his diet. He could lose a few pounds, but at least he doesn't smoke."

Marty returned his smile tremulously. "Thank you, Doctor. I feel much better."

The next day Rick drove Marty home from her father's house in brooding silence. Vera had remained there to keep him company.

Rick could postpone his trip to Reno no longer. Marty had assured him several times that she would understand if he had to go, but he hated to leave her. He wished she could be with him, but of course she had to stay close to her father and run the business.

Rick waited until they were sitting on the living room couch before mentioning his departure. Marty brought two glasses of wine and curled up next to him.

"He's so much better already," she remarked, sipping absently. "I can see the color returning to his face."

"Yes," Rick said, stroking her golden hair. "I can see the color returning to yours too."

Marty smiled and turned her cheek to his caressing fingers. Rick had been wonderful during the whole ordeal. It would have been much more grueling without his quiet strength to lean on.

"If you really think you'll be okay, I've put off my trip about as long as I can," he said, watching her closely.

"Oh." She knew that he wouldn't go unless he really had to, but she'd allowed herself to be lulled into relying on his presence.

Her sometimes prickly sense of independence came to her rescue when tears threatened to fill her eyes. It wouldn't do to make a habit of counting on Rick. Despite the fact that they had grown even closer over the last few days, and Marty's love was deeper than ever, Rick had remained silent on the subject of his feelings toward her.

"I understand," she said quickly. "You must know how much I've appreciated having you here."

His eyes crinkled as he smiled down at her, tucked into the curve of his arm. "Believe me, being with you has been no hardship. I wish I didn't have to go at all, but they're expecting me to conduct a seminar on sales practices tomorrow afternoon. I have a tentative reservation first thing in the morning, if you're sure you'll be all right."

In nonverbal answer to his question, Marty set down the empty wineglass and tangled her fingers in his dark hair. Reaching up, she rubbed his lips lightly with her own, then let her tongue trace the sensual curve of his lower lip, teasing her way into the dark recesses beyond.

Feeling his hard shudder of response, she trailed the fingers of one hand from his nape around to the button at the top of his shirt. Rick's hands clamped on her waist as she opened the garment enough to gain access to the flat muscles of his chest. When her fingers searched through the light covering of hair to find one small male nipple, his skin rippled in response. Discovering the tiny bud, she lowered her mouth and caressed it with her tongue.

A harsh moan rumbled from somewhere deep in Rick's chest. Shifting abruptly, he pushed Marty onto the wide cushions of the couch, following with his now aroused body. His mouth covered hers in a rough, passionate kiss and then one of his big hands slid in between their straining bodies. In seconds he'd opened the front of her blouse and unhooked the lacy bra.

141

Marty's back arched as he took the pouting tip of one breast deep within his mouth. He drew on it rhythmically, making her body pulsate wildly.

Sliding her hand down his muscular belly, she pushed questing fingers under his wide leather belt. When he'd sucked in his breath, her hand reached farther.

Moments after her daring assault, their clothing lay in a heap on the floor and Rick's mouth and hands were exploring her most sensitive places. As her thighs fell open in helpless surrender, he positioned himself and thrust deeply.

The pace of Marty's body matched his as they soared in a passionate flight that became more magical even as it became more familiar. They glided to a peak of satisfaction that was higher every time they made love.

As their hearts and bodies began a slow recovery, Marty remembered Rick's impending departure. How she would miss him while he was gone! She had really hoped that they would find the time in Reno to work out some of the things that lay between them, dormant and misunderstood.

The question of her retirement hadn't come up again, and neither had the all-star tour. She had to give her answer to the coach soon, and now she had run out of time to make Rick see how important it was.

The honor of traveling with the hand-picked team wasn't one to be taken lightly. If her father's health permitted, she wanted very much to go. Rick would just have to understand.

He carried Marty into the bedroom, her arms twined about his neck. Their gazes met and held.

"Can you stay with me?" she asked, wanting to

spend every possible moment with him before he left.

He shook his head reluctantly as he set her on her feet and pulled back the covers of her bed. "My plane leaves at six A.M. I have to go home first to pack some things."

Marty's fingers closed around his wrist. "Stay for a while," she begged, pulling him downward. "I'll set the alarm."

Before Rick dialed her number from his hotel room the next evening, he tried to shake off the questions that plagued him. Perhaps if Marty had been able to go with him, they would have had time to talk things out. The idea that she could look forward to being away from him for a whole month still rankled. It would be easier to accept if he knew what her plans were for next season.

Marty traveled in her job, to fairs and trade shows as well as in delivering and setting up the greenhouses. So did Rick, to a certain degree. He also coached a boys' Little League team each spring, and sponsored two soccer teams in the fall. He'd even accepted Marty's working relationship with that blond beach bum, and he wondered with a wicked grin if Marty would be as understanding if Mavis traveled with *him*. He thought not, feeling smug and superior.

Their schedules could be worked out, but not if she was also going to continue playing. It wasn't only the out-of-town tournaments; it was turnouts, league games, pitching practice to keep her arm in shape.

Softball didn't run just for three months in the summer; there was much more to it than that, especially for a top pitcher like Marty. Her commitment was likely to begin in January with indoor workouts and run through September if the team advanced through the play-offs again. If Marty didn't retire they'd never be together, he thought with a fierce scowl.

His frown deepened when her phone rang eight times with no answer. She was probably either at her father's or still at work. How could she possibly consider taking off for a month to gallop around the country when he was ill? She hadn't hesitated to skip the Reno trip, Rick thought with a muttered expletive.

No, that was unfair. She had to stay; her father needed her. Rick slammed a fist down on the wood-grained nightstand. Dammit, he needed her too. He was only beginning to realize just how much. Stringing together a line of curses he hadn't used since his baseball days, he grabbed a sport coat and stomped out of his room.

For Marty, the days until Rick returned dragged with agonizing slowness, even though she was kept busy running the business and visiting her father. Rick called almost every night, but they never spoke of the things that weighed heavily between them. A couple of evenings he didn't call, and Marty tortured herself with images of him pursuing glamorous casino queens, with visions of his sexy body wrapped in the arms of some woman much more sophisticated than herself.

Roasting upon the spit of her own jealous imaginings, Marty began to better understand Rick's disgruntled remarks about her friendship with Jerry. She'd finally convinced Rick that Jerry was just someone she worked with. Of course, Jerry's new found and total dedication to Pauline lent

144

Marty's explanation more authenticity than anything Marty herself could have said.

When she'd mentioned Rick's slinky receptionist in an attempt at retaliation, he'd thrown back his head and burst into laughter. She had yet to interpret *that* reaction, but could see that bringing Mavis into any future discussions about possible grounds for jealousy would be entirely pointless.

Early Friday evening Marty stomped into her apartment, her mood as dark and cloudy as her eyes. Rick hadn't called the evening before, and she'd been out on a job all day. According to her calculations, he should be back tomorrow.

She tossed a frozen dinner into the microwave and headed for the shower, shedding clothes as she went. At the time it didn't matter that she would just have to pick them up later. The small act of rebellion made her feel slightly better.

Drying off quickly after the shower, she pulled on a snug, worn velour robe and padded back to the kitchen. She stepped over the jeans that lay on the hall floor in an untidy heap with the same naughty grin she might have worn as a child doing it.

The chicken and rice dinner in its plastic tray held no more appeal than it had when it was still frozen. Marty studied it for a long moment before sliding the whole concoction into the trash. Too bad she hadn't asked Jerry to stop for a pizza.

How could she forget that he had a date with Pauline. All Marty had heard during the fairly complex job they'd done that afternoon was Pauline this and Pauline that. It was almost enough to make her wish that she hadn't helped to get them together.

145

Not that either one had ever given her any credit for it, she remembered with a disdainful sniff. They both acted as if what had happened at Rick's party had been choreographed by God, not Marty Gibson.

Marty grinned to herself, pulling a diet Pepsi from the fridge and opening it. Did she act as nauseatingly as the two of them? Suddenly she slammed down the soda can as a horrid thought crossed her mind. Perhaps she did, and that was why Rick hadn't phoned the night before. He was through with her.

Oh, how she wished he would call! Taking the soft drink into the living room, she glared balefully at the silent phone. She sank onto the couch, clutching the satin pillow from Atlantic City to her middle as if it were a long lost teddy bear.

Finally realization began to penetrate her fog of self-pity. If she was this discombobulated after less than a week, what kind of shape would she be in if she was gone for a month with the all-star team?

Frowning and sipping the cold drink, she finally came to the decision she'd been wrestling with since that exciting telephone call had come the week before.

As she hung up the receiver a few moments later, the doorbell pealed loudly. Expecting no one, she tightened the belt of her robe and peered cautiously through the peephole. There wasn't anyone there. Puzzled, she opened the door and stepped into the hallway. Before she could utter a word, a big, devastatingly handsome male grabbed her and covered her surprised mouth with a mind-blowing kiss.

"Good Lord, I missed you," Rick said, voice thick with passion held way too long in check. His

146

dark head lowered to find Marty's mouth again, and the door across the hall opened a crack. One brown eye stared at them.

"Come inside," Marty urged, grabbing his arm. "Evening, Mr. Ridgeway," she called past Rick's shoulder. The door across the hall shut with a thud that managed somehow to sound disapproving.

She pulled Rick inside and launched herself into his waiting arms. Dimly, above the roaring in her ears, she heard her own door slam shut. For several moments she contented herself with kissing his mouth, his cheeks, his eyelids, and his throat right beneath his ear, her hands locked around his neck to hold his head still. Then the realization that he hadn't called her the night before, and that he wasn't supposed to be home until sometime the next day, intruded, and she shoved him abruptly away.

"Hey!" His breathing was shallow, his sexy lower lip looked slightly fuller than usual, and there was a dull red flush across his face.

"What happened?" he asked as she placed her hands on her hips and glared at him. "My welcome home was going great there, and all of a sudden, bam." He tipped his head to one side in puzzlement.

"What are you doing here?" Marty demanded. "You're supposed to be in Reno."

"You want me to go back?" Puzzlement was rapidly replaced by irritation.

Marty's mouth opened and shut. To her horror, tears filled her eyes and threatened to spill onto her cheeks. He was here, in the flesh, and she was ruining his surprise. Chagrin and guilt swamped her. She felt just terrible.

Rick saw the suspicious sheen and immediately

leapt to the wrong conclusion. "Oh, my God," he exclaimed. "Is your father all right?" His fingers curled around Marty's upper arms as he stared down into her face.

She nodded her head and the slight movement caused the tears to roll down her cheeks.

"Is the business okay?"

Her head bobbed again, more tears streaming down her cheeks.

He was silent, wracking his brain. What else was there? Just when he'd decided that she wasn't one of those kooky women whose moods went up and down like a yo-yo . . . All he had wanted to do was surprise her.

"Marty!" His voice was sharp, startling them both. "What's wrong?" All the helpless male frustration he felt in the face of women's tears welled up in his voice.

To Marty it sounded just like irritation.

"I m-missed you," she wailed, feeling utterly ridiculous.

Her words cut through Rick's heart like a hot knife through a slab of butter. He dropped the bag he'd been holding and took her in his arms, cuddling her head under his chin.

"Sweetie, I missed you too," he murmured into her golden hair. Emotion bubbled deep within him. He'd been totally frustrated the evening before, trapped by a long-winded colleague until it was too late to call.

After tossing and turning for a couple of hours, he'd been tempted to phone her anyway. Only the knowledge that she needed her sleep to run her father's business had kept him from waking her. Instead, he'd done the next best thing—called the airport at first light and hopped a plane home a day early.

Only that same self-control enabled him to sit on the couch and pull her onto his lap instead of leading her directly to the bedroom.

"I'm here a day early," he said tenderly. "Doesn't that prove how much I missed you?"

Marty hiccupped softly, refusing to meet his eyes. Her head dipped in a silent nod as he handed her a neatly folded handkerchief.

Then she spied a paper bag on the carpet where Rick had dropped it. "What's that?"

"For you," he said as he tossed it casually onto her lap. "A souvenir from the biggest little city in the world."

Marty chuckled with delight as she pulled out a lime-green satin pillow bordered with silky fringe. A picture of two dice was painted on the front in black and white, and pasted-on rhinestones formed the word *Reno.*

"What a perfect set this will make with my Atlantic City pillow," she exclaimed, pulling the pink satin confection from the corner of the couch.

"That's what I thought." Playfully, Rick held a hand over his eyes as if the glare from the two fluorescent cushions was too bright. "Have you eaten yet?" he asked after she thanked him with a kiss.

She shook her head.

"Neither have I. Put some clothes on and come with me."

As soon as Marty emerged from the bedroom, Rick shoved her purse into her hands, grabbed a jacket from the closet, wrapped it around her shoulders, and walked her to the door.

Speeding along in the black Mercedes, Marty

blew her nose again, checked her mascara for damage in the small mirror from her purse, and turned to the man who filled the car with his masculine presence.

"Where are you taking me?" she asked in a small voice, feelings of joy, embarrassment, love, and desire all tumbled together inside her.

When their gazes locked, the expression on Rick's face wiped away all her embarrassment, leaving only joy, desire, and love. "Home," he said, reaching for her hand and cradling it in one of his.

Upon arrival, the next place he headed after taking his luggage down the hallway was the kitchen. She didn't say a word when he pulled the exact kind of frozen dinner she had dumped earlier from his large freezer.

"These okay?" he asked. "I'm afraid the fridge is almost bare."

"Oh, fine," she answered. "But I could have fixed you something at my place."

Rick put the trays in the microwave. "I wanted us to be here," he said over his shoulder as he dug around in the fridge and produced a bottle of white wine.

"You didn't eat on the plane?"

He snorted derisively. "If you call that dinner."

While they consumed the dinners and drank the bottle of wine, Rick told Marty about his trip and she brought him up to date on her father's progress. Not once did he mention any fast women or wild parties. It sounded as if he'd been busy every minute with the convention, renewing old acquaintances from all over the country.

"I hope that you can come next year," he said. "I was looking forward to showing you off."

At his words, Marty's heart almost popped from her chest in sheer happiness. It sure didn't sound as if he was beginning to tire of her.

"I almost forgot!" she exclaimed suddenly, remembering her phone conversation moments before his arrival at her apartment. "I talked to the coach from the all-star team right before you arrived."

Rick's eyes narrowed and he set down his wineglass. "And?" he probed.

Marty slid back her chair and stood. "And," she murmured, voice dropping seductively as she snuggled onto his lap, feeling his instant response to her shifting movements. "I turned down the trip," she finished only seconds before her lips met his.

The sensuality of the scene evaporated with Rick's shocked reaction. "You what?" he exclaimed, jumping to his feet, spilling his wine, nearly upsetting the table, and allowing Marty to slide to an ignominious heap on the floor.

"Help me up!" she sputtered.

"Sorry."

When she was standing again, rubbing at her bruised bottom with one hand, she decided to try again. "I turned down the tour."

"That's what I thought you said. Why? Because of your father?"

"No, dummy," she answered, knowing that her eyes revealed much more than she wanted him to see. "I did it for us. I couldn't stand the thought of being separated from you again so soon."

"Oh, babe," Rick muttered, voice raw with some emotion Marty couldn't identify. He swept her into his arms. "I missed you too, but I know how much you were looking forward to playing on the all-stars."

"Not nearly as much as I was looking forward to your coming home," Marty murmured as Rick's mouth descended.

After a long kiss, sanity slowly returned. "How about a dip?" he asked, eyes dark with passion.

"A dip?" Marty echoed, glancing out the window to his pool. "I don't know. It looks cold out there and I don't have a suit."

Tossing his head back to laugh delightedly, Rick ran a long finger down her cheek. "The hot tub," he murmured, breath tickling Marty's ear. "No suits."

"Oh, I see."

Moments later, after a ritual of undressing each other that almost resulted in a detour to the master suite's huge bed, Marty slid into warm, soothing water. The hot tub took up most of a small room done in tile and redwood. It was off the main bedroom, separated from the outdoors by sliding glass walls and slatted shades.

"We could fix you up with more energy-efficient glass for this room," Marty mused, glancing around. Self-consciousness had hit unexpectedly, causing her to look anywhere but at Rick's gloriously nude male body as he walked across the tile floor and settled next to her.

"Can we discuss that later?" he asked, one hand turning her face to his. "Right now there's a fantasy I want to play out."

"A fantasy?" The words ended somewhere between a squeak and a giggle as Marty's breath caught in her throat. The expression on Rick's face was devastating in its intensity. She slid lower in the water.

"A fantasy that ran through my head every night I was away from you," he rumbled, pulling her up to him as his lips caught hers in a kiss that she was sure cracked the polish on her toenails.

Marty had heard about love scenes in hot tubs. She'd even read a book about a murder in one. The things Rick was doing to her willing body made her feel she'd died and gone to heaven. His talented mouth licked and tasted her, beginning with her chin and the lobes of her ears. By the time he'd worked his way to the hardened tips of her breasts, drawing on one with his mouth and tormenting the other with his fingertips, her eyes were squeezed shut and her mind a blank.

Marty's hands stroked his arms restlessly, then moved over the wet skin of his shoulders and across his chest. When one hand slid beneath the warm water, down his ribs and then through the coarser hair below his navel, Rick began to lose track of what he was doing.

"I need you." His voice was thick with passion barely held in check. For a moment his fingers caressed her intimately and Marty arched against him. Then his hands splayed across her hips and he settled her upon him.

Marty's legs hugged him as he filled her. Supported by the water's buoyancy and Rick's hands, she moved her hips in slow undulation.

Breath hissed through his gritted teeth and a hard shudder racked him. He pressed her closer, taking control. Marty felt the world begin to shatter as the rhythm of their loving changed and deepened, leaving nothing but a tidal wave of feelings building within her.

The cry that left her parted lips was the final spur to Rick's own release. Arching upward, he surrendered himself totally.

CHAPTER NINE

Rick wrapped Marty in a huge green bath towel and then scooped her into his arms. Her eyes were smoky as she gazed up at him, a sleepy smile of fulfillment on her swollen lips.

A strong emotion he could no longer fail to identify swept over him as he cradled her to his chest. For weeks he'd fenced with the knowledge that this fabulous creature had taken possession of his heart. It was time to admit the truth, to himself and to her.

"I'm so glad you're back," Marty murmured, tangling her fingers in the damp hair at the nape of his neck.

"And I'm sorry I had to leave you while your father was still so ill," Rick countered. "I missed you terribly." He carried her into the huge master suite and sat on the edge of the king-sized bed, still holding her.

"Are you sure about the all-star team?" he asked, unwrapping her like a Christmas present. "It's a lot to give up."

Marty's breathing became more rapid as one of his large hands fitted itself over her breast.

154

"I wanted to," she gasped as he inclined his head, tongue stroking the hardening nipple. "I can't bear to think of us separated for all that time."

"I can't stand to think of us being separated at all," Rick said, carefully rewrapping the towel as Marty groaned with frustration and tugged at the hair on his chest. His hand tipped her chin so they were staring into each other's eyes.

Now that he had her full attention, he found it difficult to force the words he wanted to say past the lump that had formed in his throat. He swallowed, then wet his lips.

Marty let her gaze slide to his mouth. She waited for his kiss. When it didn't come, puzzlement filled her eyes. What was wrong?

Rick lifted her from his lap and moved them both back into the softness of the big bed. He seemed totally unconcerned by his own nudity and Marty did her best to ignore it.

Unfortunately, her body wasn't cooperating. Her hand slid down his chest and skimmed over stomach muscles that rippled under her soft touch. Before her questing fingers could reach their goal, Rick manacled her wrist in an iron grasp.

"Hungry little baggage, aren't you?" He teased. "Here I am trying to propose, and you're more interested in my body."

Marty stiffened at his casual words. "W-what?" Her eyes widened as she looked into his smiling face, stunned.

Rick propped himself on one elbow and leaned over her. "I'm asking you to marry me."

Marty frowned. "I wasn't even sure that you love me. Do you?"

155

"Oh, hell," Rick grumbled. "You know that I love you, just like I know that you love me." His gaze slid away and he plucked at the bedspread with his fingers.

"Tell me." A slow smile pulled at Marty's lips as bubbles of happiness welled up inside her. "I want the words, Rick." She found his nervousness delightfully endearing.

After a moment an answering smile lighted up Rick's face, a smile of such sweetness that tears filled Marty's eyes. "I love you," he murmured tenderly. "I haven't said those words to a woman since I was eleven years old, unless you want to count my mother." His hand brushed the hair back from her forehead and he placed a gentle kiss against her temple.

"I'll always love you, and I want you for my wife."

A tear spilled down Marty's cheek and he caught it with the tip of his tongue. Her arms wrapped around his neck and she pulled him to her.

He resisted. "Will you?" he asked again.

"Yes," she answered. "Oh, yes, yes, yes."

A sigh of relief left his lips that just before they covered hers in a kiss filled with possession and joy.

Sometime later Marty lay snuggled against Rick's warmth, one hand idly tracing patterns on his broad chest. Softly she blew on the light dusting of dark hair.

"Let's make it soon," he said. "As soon as your father is able to be there."

"Can you wait a month?" Marty asked in a teasing voice. "I would like the time to make some arrangements. Something small but special."

156

He nodded slowly. "I guess a month would be okay. I hope that Karen and her family will be able to come out. I'm sure my folks won't mind leaving their retirement home in Florida long enough to see their only son get married."

For a few moments the room was silent as Rick kissed her and murmured sweet nonsense into her ear.

Then he sat up. "I've decided to sponsor the team again next year," he said. "Do you think Pat will be able to find a couple of pitchers?"

Marty sat up too, tucking the sheet around herself. "Why a couple?"

He smiled expansively. "It would be nice to have three on the roster, the way Louise's husband tends to keep her home from tournaments." Running a big hand through his hair, he continued. "I know you'll be a tough act to follow," he said as casually as if he were discussing the options on a new Mercedes, "but if she starts looking right away . . ."

Slowly the meaning of his words began to sink in. Rick expected her to retire, just as her father did. He hadn't even given her the courtesy of making up her own mind; instead, he was doing it for her. A feeling of resentment flowed through her. Just when everything should be wonderful, Rick had once again put his foot in it. He was still trying to run things.

Marty edged away from him. She couldn't believe his arrrogance, his presumption that she was through. She was willing to bet that no one had told him when to retire. Why couldn't he cut her the same slack? Perhaps she wasn't ready to walk away from all the years she'd worked so hard to get to the top.

"You're making some huge assumptions," she said, trying to keep her voice light.

Rick stopped when he saw the expression on her face. Her mouth was curved upward, but her eyes were narrowed as if he'd just suggested the team convert to slowpitch.

"What's the matter?"

Marty slid from the bed and began to search for her clothes. "Why will Pat need to replace me?" she asked in a deceptively mild tone as she turned away to dress. Of all the emotions coursing through her, disappointment was the strongest. She'd been foolish enough to think that Rick had mellowed since she first knew him. Instead, she'd stupidly given her love to a man who apparently knew nothing about sharing, only controlling.

The hair on the back of Rick's neck began to prickle, and every instinct told him that something was very wrong. "I assumed you'd be retiring," he said cautiously, "from several remarks you've made. Besides, with all the traveling you do for Gibson Enterprises, you can't play softball and be married to me."

It was entirely the wrong phrasing. He realized that when she whirled around, her face flushed and her eyes stormy. He was not to know that anger was the only way she could mask the pain she felt. Defensively, realizing that he had introduced the topic in a clumsy and tactless way, he felt his own control slip.

"Can't?" she questioned, spitting out the word as if it were a bit of sour apple. Clearly, she hadn't arrived at the same conclusion regarding her softball playing that he had. "How can you dare to assume the answer to one of the most important things in my life?"

158

Marty sucked in a deep breath. Perhaps he would say that he was mistaken, that he'd screwed up. Perhaps they could still salvage something, work through it. The flicker of hope died out when she saw the expression on his face change from wariness to arrogance.

Rick rose from the rumpled bed like Neptune from a churning sea. For a moment his nude body distracted Marty, then her eyes returned to his face. His dark brows had pulled together into a straight line, and the blue of his eyes had turned icy cold. She shivered as she buttoned her blouse, resenting the way he'd spoiled what should have been the happiest moments of her life.

"It's time for you to retire," he pressed, his voice crackling with authority. "I thought you could see that." He'd known plenty of guys who hung around the game too long. It would be better for Marty to quit while she was on top.

"I'm in my prime," she retorted, reacting to the tone of his voice. What a fool she'd been to think that Rick had changed. He was still as bossy as he'd been that first day at practice. He still assumed that his was the only right way and that he knew best for everyone. What if he was that way about anything that would take her attention away from him? Next he'd be making decisions about her career with Gibson Enterprises. Before she knew it, she'd be a passive housewife, knee-deep in babies. She shuddered.

"You're being horribly selfish," she continued. Everything was ruined and her happy mood of but moments before was being replaced rapidly by a sense of frustration and doom. It was becoming crystal-clear that they were poles apart in their expectations.

"Selfish!" he echoed. "Why? Because I want a wife, not a teammate?" He was almost shouting. "You're the selfish one."

"I won't marry someone who thinks he can tell me what to do," Marty shot back. "And I don't need another father!"

Rick's face flushed darkly at her words, and his lips thinned with anger.

Determined not to cry in front of him, she hoped desperately that her anger would carry her through until she could sort things out alone. Stepping into her shoes, she picked up her purse from where it lay on the floor.

"I'm going to call a cab," she said, needing to get away and think things out. "I don't know how you can say that I'm selfish, when I gave up the all-star tour for you." She knew that was unfair as soon as the words left her mouth. Quitting the tour had been her own choice, one that now proved to be a bad one. How many other bad choices would she make if they stayed together? Clutching the remains of her frustration to her like a ragged cloak, she turned on one heel and left the room.

As she stalked out, slamming the door behind her, Rick muttered a sharp curse and began to search for his jeans. By the time he'd found them under the bedding that had been pushed to the floor in a tangled heap and walked into the living room, Marty had made her call. She stood staring out the front window.

"Did you get a taxi?" Rick asked, not knowing what else to say. "I would have driven you home." He was stunned by the way the argument had exploded so quickly, and unsure what to do.

"I didn't want you to drive me," she snapped

160

without turning around. "My cab will be here in five minutes."

The tone of her voice made him angrier than before. She had no right to be mad, since she was the one being totally unreasonable. He kept his distance, fuming silently.

After a moment she glanced over her shoulder. If only they could discuss the situation calmly. No, she wouldn't tolerate someone telling her how to run her life. She'd been right weeks ago. He was overbearing and arrogant, and she had just missed making a horrible mistake. Since she was doing the right thing, why did she already feel so miserable?

Watching the mutinous expression on her oval face, Rick realized that he had jumped to some unfounded conclusions. Marty wasn't about to change her life-style for him. Angrily, he jammed his hands into the pockets of his low-slung jeans, balling them into fists.

"I guess you won't have to worry about those arrangements," he snarled. "We've both had a narrow escape."

Marty flinched at the words. Hearing them spoken out loud hurt terribly. She had hoped that they could work things out after they had both cooled off, but pride forced her to agree with him.

"That's right," she said, glad for the anger that gave her voice strength. "The wedding is off. We'll just pretend you never proposed, okay?"

His face held a harshness that cost him a great deal, but she couldn't know it did. "Right," he agreed.

Since her father's release from the hospital, Marty had developed the habit of spending a considerable amount of time with him. She usually stopped by there after work, then left when Vera arrived to fix his dinner. That way Marty kept him informed about the business.

Gradually, over the week he'd been home, their conversations had drifted into other areas. At first Marty was uncomfortable when he began to talk about her childhood. Then his memories of life before her mother had died triggered her own. Before she knew it, they were laughing at some of the things the three of them had done together. Over the years Marty had forgotten how close they'd all been, or maybe she'd deliberately thrust the memories aside. In any case, it was now time to bring them out again.

From the things he told her, Marty understood for the first time how hard it had been for him to raise a daughter alone, while mourning the wife he'd loved so much. What Marty had taken as disapproval was only his natural reserve, and his seeming disinterest in her only a lack of time because of the business he was trying to build.

The day after her fight with Rick she drove to her father's apartment. He had already been brought up to date on the business, but there was no one else she was willing to confide in.

Deep inside, Marty knew that she should hang up her cleats, but a stubborn sense of independence made her want to pick the time, not have it thrust upon her. Even though her father had said quite a bit about her retirement during the last couple of years, their new closeness made her turn to him instinctively.

Her relationship with Rick was something Mr. Gibson had refrained from mentioning since the younger man had gone to Reno. In fact, after the outrageous suggestion that they marry while they were there, he hadn't referred to Rick at all, except to ask once when he would be back. Her anger over her father's remark must have warned him that discretion would be a wiser course.

She rang the doorbell, hoping that he would be home and alone for once. It would have taken someone less observant than Marty not to notice how deeply he and Vera cared about each other. Marty just hoped the other woman wasn't there now.

The door opened and surprise touched Mr. Gibson's face, to be replaced almost instantly by a smile of pleasure.

"Martha! Come in." He stepped back and she stepped past him. "I just made a fresh pot of decaf. Will you have some?"

She glanced around the neat, Spartan apartment. "If I'm not interrupting. Where's Vera?"

He led the way to his small kitchen. "She's gone to lunch and shop with a friend. Then she and I are going to a movie this evening."

Marty accepted the steaming mug and sat down at the dinette table, noticing a bowl of fresh flowers. Now that she was here she wasn't sure how to begin. Her father sat across from her, his smile fading.

"You look tired," he said, worry darkening his expression. "I'll bet last week was too big a strain. So much responsibility thrown at you all at once."

Before Marty could interrupt, he continued in an excited tone. "You know, I always meant to get you more involved in the actual running of things, but it was easy to let it slide while you were doing such a fine job with the solar division. Adding that line was a real stroke of genius. Now I realize that it's past time to make you a full partner."

Marty's eyes widened. "Partner?" she asked.

"Jerry was by first thing this morning. He told me what a terrific job you've been doing. Of course I always knew that you'd be able to take over someday. I just didn't realize how soon someday would be."

His words left her speechless. She'd always assumed he longed for a son to follow in his footsteps; now he was saying that he planned to have her take over. Then his last words sank in.

"You're going to be running Gibson Enterprises for a long time yet," she said stoutly. "Don't be talking gloom to me when we both know what a tough old bird you are. The doctor did say that this was just a warning."

He patted her hand reassuringly. "I know. And that's one reason I want you to continue learning all about everything, so you can take over when I retire."

"Retire! When did you decide all this?" She couldn't believe that her father would willingly consider leaving the company he'd first started in his garage.

He cleared his throat and she could've sworn she actually saw a twinkle in his eye. "I made the decision right after I proposed to Vera and she accepted," he said proudly. "You know that we've been seeing a lot of each other since she asked me to escort her to Rick's party. I wanted to ask her out, but I guess I just didn't have the nerve. Thank God she did. Anyway, we want to do some traveling while we're still young!"

Marty couldn't have been more stunned if he had just announced that he was running away to

164

join the circus. It was wonderful news and she was delighted that her father had found someone as nice as Vera to share his later years. She jumped up and moved around the small table to give him a warm hug.

He stood, too, and enfolded her in his arms. Marty felt the last of the barriers between them fall away.

"Thank you for your understanding, Martha," he said. "You know that I'll always carry your mother in my heart." He paused and cleared his throat. "I love Vera in a different way, and she's a terrific woman."

Marty smiled up at him. "I'm happy for you both," she said in a voice choked with emotion. Then thoughts of his coming marriage reminded her of what had happened between Rick and herself. Without warning, tears filled her eyes. As Marty fought for control, painful sobs welled up, shaking her with their intensity.

For a moment Mr. Gibson stiffened in surprise. Then his embrace became comforting and he patted her shoulder. "Care to tell Dad about it?" he asked as he led her into the living room and sat her on the couch. "Is it thinking about your mother that makes you sad?"

Marty shook her head, dabbing at her eyes with the handkerchief Gordon pulled from his shirt pocket. After she had poured out a censored version of her breakup with Rick, her father rose and fetched them both more coffee.

"That boy's been a celebrity in Allentown since way before he quit playing baseball," he commented, sipping the dark brew. "He's cut quite a wide swath socially too."

Marty wasn't sure what he was getting at. "I

suppose that's true," she said, frowning. Rick would probably return to the freewheeling bachelor existence he'd enjoyed before they'd met, with hardly a backward glance. The thought brought fresh tears to her eyes, and she dabbed at them with the damp linen.

"It was a big step for him to propose," Mr. Gibson continued.

"If you're going to tell me how lucky I am—" Marty began hotly.

"No, honey. I was just thinking about how much Rick has changed over the last weeks. I'm surprised that someone like him would want to get tied down, even to a wonderful girl like my daughter. And from what you told me before, he really looked down on your team. Now you say he's going to sponsor them next year. It sounds like he's come around quite a bit in his attitude."

Marty glared into her coffee cup. "Maybe so," she said. "But he still thinks he can run my life. Nobody tells me when to quit softball. That's my decision."

He sighed and leaned back, stretching his arm along the top of the couch. "That's probably my fault," he said. "I nagged you so much about quitting that when Rick mentioned it, I'll bet you just blew."

Standing up, she shook her head, unconsciously thrusting out her chin. "He has to accept me the way I am," she argued. "I'm not going to turn into someone with no mind of her own just to please a man."

"It seems to me that he's changed quite a bit for you," Mr. Gibson commented in a mild tone, finishing his coffee.

"He's not giving up anything! I'm the one who

166

has to make the sacrifices," Marty all but shouted. Even as the words left her mouth, she wondered if they were entirely true.

Several days later she was still wondering. Rick had a devastating way of invading her thoughts, no matter where she was or what she was doing. Every time the doubts began to creep in, she reviewed in her mind his hopelessly arrogant attitude. She remembered how he'd acted when she first suggested he sponsor a women's team, and his bossiness when he showed up at turnout.

Now he wanted her to fit into some slot he'd chosen for his future wife. As she dashed her signature across checks for several of Gibson's suppliers, she reminded herself yet again what a narrow escape she'd had.

It didn't help that her body missed Rick's loving with a raw hunger that left her tossing and turning at night and aching with need during the day. Marty wondered if they would ever resolve their differences so they could again share the delights of two people perfectly attuned. If not, the spot in her heart that Rick had filled so completely would remain ever empty. The hope that he would come to his senses and call her faded with each day that passed.

One afternoon, when she and Jerry had both finished up early, Marty walked over to his truck as he was unlocking the door. Busy with managing the business, and preoccupied with her own misery, Marty hadn't really talked to Jerry in days. After she'd chewed him out over a screwed-up delivery, he'd done his best to avoid her.

He looked up as she stopped beside him. "Hi,"

he said cautiously, as if he expected another lecture.

"Hi," Marty echoed. He waited as she tried to think of something else to say. "We haven't been out for pizza in a long time," she finally ventured. "How about grabbing one tonight? My treat."

"I'm sorry, Marty. I can't." A blush spread across his cheeks, something she hadn't seen since he and Pauline had become so close.

"I've, uh, got other plans tonight," he continued, not meeting her eyes.

"Oh, of course." Marty felt as if her smile was glued on. "Pauline?"

"Yeah. I'm, uh, moving into her place and she's cooking dinner."

Marty couldn't help but grin at his acute discomfort. "I'm glad," she managed to say, patting his arm. "It sounds like things are going really well for you two."

"Yeah. Pauline's crazy about my body-building. She goes to all the competitions."

For a moment they fell silent as each remembered how Marty used to go with him, and their easy friendship. She sighed. Nothing stayed the same.

"I'm sorry about you and Rick," he said. "Your dad told me that you broke up."

"Thanks," Marty almost whispered, wondering when the pain would begin to ease. She shrugged and tried to smile. "It just didn't work out."

Jerry touched her arm. "Say," he exclaimed. "Why don't you come over to Pauline's with me. I know she's fixed extra spaghetti, and she's a great cook."

Marty's sense of humor was restored as she shook her head, knowing that her presence that evening would be as welcome as fleas at a cat show. Jerry still had a lot to learn about women. "Thanks, but I wouldn't be very good company."

After a moment he nodded, blue eyes clouded with concern. "Yeah, I understand. But you gotta come by and see us soon, okay?"

Marty agreed. After a couple of silent moments he glanced at his watch. "Well, I better be going. I still have some stuff to pack. You okay?"

Marty forced herself to smile brightly. "Of course. You go on now. I'll see you tomorrow." As Jerry drove off, she wondered if she had ever felt so very much alone.

After a week had crawled by and Rick had made no effort to get in touch with her, Marty knew she had to accept the fact that it was truly over between them. There was no way she could go to him, unless she was willing to sacrifice a part of herself to fit the role he wanted her to play. If she did that, eventually her love would die of suffocation. Once the pattern was set, there would be other things Rick would expect her to give in on. She couldn't risk it. Apparently his ideal of the perfect wife was more important to him than Marty's love.

Making the company bank deposit the next Friday, she looked up to find him staring at her from the other side of the lobby. His face was expressionless as they studied each other for a timeless moment—but he looked fatigued. Then he turned away to shake the hand of one of the senior bank officials.

Marty's heartbeat quickened to double time as she waited for Rick to approach. It didn't seem possible or fair that he looked even more handsome than she remembered in the same double-breasted, pin-striped suit he'd been wearing the very first time they met in his office.

Marty swallowed nervously, trying to think of something to say to him. The man in line ahead of her finished his business at the teller's window and Marty moved up. When she looked back to Rick he was already going out the door, his hand cupping the elbow of his curvaceous, redheaded secretary. A feeling of real hopelessness stole over Marty with the realization that she and Rick were no longer even friends.

Rick's hand was still shaking as he unlocked the car door for Mavis. Seeing Marty at the bank had caught him unprepared for the stab of pain that skewered his gut, even though he knew they were bound to run into each other sometime. Allentown wasn't all that big.

"I saw her too," Mavis said to him as they drove back to the agency.

"Who?" Even as he tried to bluff, Rick knew he'd failed.

"Come off it, boss. Your tan faded like cheap carpeting when you spotted her in that line."

Mavis spoke like the longtime friend she was. "Why don't you swallow that prickly male pride that's sticking in your throat and fix the situation before your whole staff mutinies?"

Rick's grin was bitter. "Are you trying to tell me that I've been a bear to work for lately?"

She smiled. "Trying?" she echoed. "I should take out a billboard. Even grizzlies would be fun to deal with compared to what you've put us all through since you and Marty broke up."

Mavis chuckled. "I knew when she first came in with the phony story about collecting for charity

170

that you'd have problems with that one," she said. Then the smile left her perfectly made-up face. "I just wish it had turned out differently," she added quietly, reaching across the expanse of black leather upholstery to pat his hand.

"So do I," Rick agreed, pain tearing at him. "So do I."

After dropping Mavis at her car in the agency's back lot, he climbed the stairs to his office to look over the computer printout listing the next shipment of new cars. It only took a few minutes for him to realize that he wasn't going to get any work done that evening.

Visions of Marty danced in his head—Marty laughing, Marty frowning in concentration, Marty with eyes full of love, face flushed with passion.

A cry of anguish sliced across the silence of his private office. With a jerk into awareness, Rick realized that the sound had come from him. His hand reached for the phone, then stopped.

There wasn't room in her life for him, he reminded himself as he raked his fingers through his hair, disrupting its dark waves. For a while he'd believed he had found the perfect woman. She was tough and vulnerable, courageous and delightfully unsure of herself at times, independent and stubborn, passionate and intelligent. Now it seemed that some of those very traits he had come to love were keeping them apart.

Were his wishes that unreasonable? He knew the schedule she would have to keep if she continued to play. Add that to weekends spent at fairs and trade shows selling solar windows, while he stayed in Allentown overseeing the agency . . .

Idly twirling a pencil, he reached back to remember how he'd known it was time to walk away

171

from baseball and start another phase of his life. His skills hadn't begun to fade, his body hadn't overwhelmed him with new aches and pains. The bat had more hits left in it, and no one seriously challenged his spot on the roster.

Somehow he'd just known. The traveling became tiresome, the pressure more than he wanted to deal with. The game was no longer the fun it had been in the early years.

He tried to equate Marty's situation with his own. Even though he now understood more clearly the dedication and ambition of the amateur female athlete, their situations weren't the same.

Marty still had a career, with Gibson Enterprises. That, added to her ball playing, left no room for him. Rick faced those facts and it hurt like hell.

Glancing at his watch, he dialed the number of Don Weeble, the man who'd umpired the pitching duel with Marty.

"Hi, cookie," he said into the receiver when Don's oldest daughter answered. "It's Uncle Rick. Is Don there? I wanted to see about inviting myself over for potluck."

The pencil in his hand doodled on the printout as he listened to her reply. The last thing he was in the mood to hear was that Don and his wife were spending a romantic getaway weekend at some honeymoon lodge in the Pocono Mountains. Even old Don's love life was in better shape than his own.

After he hung up the phone, he spent several minutes trying to erase the skull and crossbones he'd drawn on the new car report. If Mavis saw that, the busybody would give him no peace.

CHAPTER TEN

Marty cradled the telephone receiver to her ear and spread garlic butter on a skinny loaf of French bread. Vera and Gordon would be there any minute, and she was waiting for Vicky to take a breath so she could cut into the woman's monologue. For some reason, rehashing the past season held no appeal. It felt as though softball had been over for months, when it really had only been a few weeks. But Marty's life had done somersaults during those weeks. Vicky's disembodied voice continued to enthuse over each detail of the team's upcoming banquet while Marty wrapped the bread in foil and checked the bubbling lasagna through the oven window.

"Yes, I think that would be fine," she agreed in response to Vicky's question about style of dress for the banquet. "I'm sure everyone would appreciate wearing casual clothes."

She listened for a moment longer as Vicky outlined the arrangements for a hall and catering. "Sounds like you've thought of everything," Marty said, glancing at her watch. She really had to get off the phone.

"What about Rick?" Apparently Vicky hadn't heard about her breakup with him. The team grapevine was usually more efficient.

"Uh, I think it would be better if you had Pauline call him," Marty said into the receiver. "Look, Vicky, I wish I had time to explain. The truth is, Dad and Vera are going to be here any minute."

As if on cue, the doorbell rang.

"Yep, they're getting married."

The doorbell rang again.

"I gotta go. Thanks for telling me about the party." She nodded impatiently as the doorbell rang for a third time. "Yeah, see you later."

Vera and Gordon both looked relieved when she finally yanked the door open.

"Sorry," she apologized as she took Vera's jacket. "The phone—" She gestured helplessly. After she'd stowed the wrap in the closet and exclaimed over the bottle of Lambrusco her father had brought, she gave Vera a hug.

"I'm so happy for you both." The dinner was her way of celebrating their upcoming nuptials. She wanted Vera to understand how much she really approved of the match.

They'd already decided to have a quiet ceremony two weeks from Saturday, the day after the softball team banquet. Marty was going to act as her father's witness, and an old friend was standing up for Vera.

Dinner was festive, punctuated with talk of all the places the older couple planned to visit after Marty took over the running of Gibson Enterprises. Gordon had informed her that he was sticking around for six months while she learned the ropes. After that he would only work part-time and she would be running the company. It would be interesting to see how well that setup worked. Nothing was said about the time she'd need to take off for softball.

Rick's name didn't come up until dessert, even though Marty had been prepared throughout dinner for the intrusion. Her stomach muscles tensed when her father asked if she'd heard anything. Marty shook her head.

"I guess Stokes isn't as bright as I first gave him credit for," Gordon said, sipping his herb tea.

Marty frowned at his words, and repressed the impulse to leap to Rick's defense. "Oh?" she said in what she hoped was a bored tone.

"I got to thinking about what you told me," Gordon continued with a glance at Vera. Marty was so intent on his words that she missed the conspiratorial light in his eyes. "You said that he's going to sponsor the team next year."

"That's right."

"Considering how difficult good sponsors are to come by, it's safe to assume that the team might fold if he hadn't stepped forward."

Marty absently stirred her coffee. "Oh, I don't know. We did come in second at the Nationals, you know."

"You're still a women's team," Gordon returned dryly. "And facts are facts. It's extremely hard to find a sponsor willing to put out the bucks for all the expenses."

"I suppose you're right," Marty admitted, glancing at Vera. "Not everyone is as generous and far-sighted as your fiancée."

The two women exchanged brief smiles.

"But I don't understand why that makes Rick less than smart," Marty said to her father.

"If he didn't sponsor the team, he could assume

175

that it would fold and you'd retire rather than start over with another group."

"So?"

Mr. Gibson took a forkful of apple cake, chewing it slowly before he continued. "Seems strange, that's all," he finally said.

Marty was still thinking about what her father had said long after he and Vera had gone and she'd placed the last dirty dish in the washer. How easy it would have been for Rick to hold off on the sponsorship, putting pressure on the team, and on Marty herself.

Would she have retired rather than start over with a new group of women, perhaps on one of the teams in Philadelphia? Why had he made it so easy for her to stay in softball? Would she really be ready to start another season in a few months, or was she just being stubborn and hanging on to something she no longer wanted? Marty pondered those questions and others, far into the night.

It was midmorning the next day when Rick glanced up from inspecting a Seville that was ready to go on the floor, to see Pauline and Jerry approaching. He greeted them with an easy smile that disguised his inner tension. He would have liked to ask them if they had seen Marty, and how she was doing. He had almost called her several times, before deciding it would be pointless.

After exchanging pleasantries, Pauline invited him to the team banquet. Rick frowned, fingering a gold pen that protruded from the pocket of his dark suit coat.

"I don't know if you've heard," he said in an expressionless voice, "but Marty and I are no longer seeing each other."

"I heard that, and I'm really sorry," Pauline said.

"But it's not as Marty's escort that we're inviting you. You're sponsoring the team next year, and you really should be there."

Jerry nodded his agreement. "It's traditional," he said.

Rick glowered at them as he searched his brain for a surefire excuse to miss the party. Nothing came to mind. "I don't know," he finally muttered. "I'll have to check my calendar."

"It's far enough away to plan around," Pauline said briskly. "We all want you there."

Rick's smile was grim. That was questionable. There was one blond pitcher who could probably do without his presence. She'd made no effort to contact him, so nothing had changed.

"I'll see what I can do," he compromised. Perhaps he'd break his leg or leave the country before the day of the banquet. Either would be preferable to spending an entire evening in the same room as Marty Gibson.

"We'll expect you," Pauline said as Jerry touched her arm. Perhaps the younger man sensed the futility of trying to push Rick into something he clearly didn't want to do.

Pauline shook off Jerry's hand. "It will ruin the party for us all if you can't make it," she continued. "Can we count on you?"

Rick's voice showed traces of exasperation, even as he admired her persistence. "I'll do my best to be there," he said. "That's all I can say."

"Great," Jerry said before Pauline could open her mouth again. "We've taken up enough of your time."

They said good-bye and Rick watched them leave the showroom. For a moment he toyed with the idea that Marty had sent Pauline, hoping for a reconciliation. Then, realizing that he was starting to fantasize, he kicked the front tire of the Seville and uttered a terse word that made one of the salesmen glance over at him in surprise.

The evening of the party Marty walked into the festively decorated hall feeling lighthearted for the first time since she and Rick had fought. One important part of her life had finally been resolved, bringing with it an inner peace that told her she'd made the right decision. She still found it amazing how very easy the choice had been once she acknowledged how empty life without Rick would be. He had grown since they'd first met, and now it was her turn. She hoped desperately that all her newfound wisdom hadn't come too late. All her doubts had been thrust aside for the evening, and there was a determined grin on Marty's face as she greeted fellow teammates and their spouses and dates.

Her pleated light-gray slacks showcased her slim hips. The blouse that she'd tucked into the pants' wide waistband was a black, gray, and white geometric print, with full sleeves gathered to tight cuffs. The silver dolphin dangled in the opening of the blouse's neckline. Her hair was an elaborate tangle of curls and her face was lightly made up. The new outfit's sophistication was supposed to give her courage to handle the challenge that awaited.

Even as she joined a laughing group who were busy dissecting the team stats that had been copied out for each player, her gaze skimmed the crowd in search of a particular dark head, a distinct set of broad shoulders. Impatience tightened her mouth when she failed to spot him.

Pauline hadn't been able to say he'd be there for

sure. Perhaps Marty was wrong and it really was too late. If that was the case, she had no one to blame but herself. It had taken time to face her shortcomings and realize that Rick had changed while she had remained selfish and obstinate. She had wanted it all, sport, career, and a future with her man. She'd known that something would have to give, but was too stubborn to face it.

Subconsciously Marty had been pushing Rick to prove over and over how much he cared. Perhaps deep inside she couldn't believe that someone as handsome, intelligent, and wonderful as he was could really love little Marty Gibson. After all, for years she'd believed that her father didn't think too much of her. With a misguided sense of self-protection, she'd pushed Rick until she had pushed him away. When she finally realized what she'd been doing, the pieces fell into place with astonishing simplicity. Now it only remained to be seen whether she'd wasted too much time in coming to her senses. If only he would be there tonight!

The first person Rick saw when he walked in the door was Marty. The pain of it slammed into his gut like a doubled-up fist, leaving him almost breathless. He'd debated about coming, before finally deciding that no stubborn blonde with more nerve than sense was going to keep him away. Now his initial reaction to the sight of her tousled hair and big gray eyes made him question whether it was worth it.

In sponsoring next year's team, he planned to remain behind the scenes. Far behind. Signing checks and putting them in the mail was as close as he was planning to get. Maybe the whole thing had been a mistake, but he'd made the offer and now he had to stick with it. He couldn't let the team down because of his own personal problems.

As several people greeted him, Rick spotted Jerry and asked him to help carry a large carton up to the stage next to the podium. As soon as they'd set it down, two of Marty's teammates began to tug at the tape holding the box shut.

"Leave it," Rick told them. "It's a surprise." By the time he'd gone out to his car and returned with another, smaller carton, dinner was being served. Habit made Rick's gaze skim the room. It settled on Marty, who was sitting at a round table with Vera, her father, Jerry, and Pauline. She looked over at Rick briefly. He glanced at the empty chair next to her and turned away.

Marty felt another claw of worry tear at her insides as Rick sat down between Vicky and Louise at a table across the room. It had been too much to hope that he would sit with her after their argument and the silence that had followed. Poking at her salad with her fork, she let the conversation among the others flow around her. After a little while a waitress took away the uneaten salad and replaced it with a plate of lasagna and Italian sausage. Try as she might, Marty was unable to keep her gaze from straying constantly to the table where Rick sat laughing and talking as if he hadn't a care in the world. After glowering at the back of his head, Marty attacked her dinner.

Even though he couldn't see her, Rick was achingly aware of Marty's presence. Self-control enabled him to joke with the others at his table and eat every bite on his plate. Meanwhile, he was dying inside.

One glimpse had been enough to make him realize that he would take Marty on any terms. He could hardly wait for the opportunity to talk to her. Somehow, they would work things out. He refused to spend the rest of his life in the kind of pain that was twisting him like a pretzel every moment they were estranged. If she wanted to play softball, he'd be in the dugout and the grandstands. There had to be a way to work it out.

As soon as the dishes were cleared, Pat approached the podium. "Before we begin the awards and distribute the trophies," she said into the microphone, "our sponsor, Rick Stokes, has a few words."

Accompanied by a hearty round of applause, Rick walked to the stage and began to tear the tape from the larger carton. "I'd thought these were gone forever," he said, pulling open the cardboard flaps.

"The missing uni's!" someone from the audience exclaimed.

Before taking anything from the box, Rick continued. "These were delivered to the high school in Pottstown with the boys' football uniforms. The summer maintenance man who signed for the delivery didn't notice that there was only supposed to be one box. He shoved them into the equipment room and they weren't discovered until the coach passed out uniforms before the first game." Rick paused to grin at the people seated in front of him. "I'm sure he was shocked." Some of them laughed in appreciation of the mystery's final solution.

"Now," he said, "I'm very pleased to be able to show you the team's new look for next year." With that he held up one of the most unattractive shirts Marty had ever seen.

The hall was silent as a tomb as Rick displayed

the top, crossed with wide horizontal stripes in turquoise, black, and white. Puzzled at the reaction, he turned it around to show the team name embroidered in black on the back.

"Oh, no," Pauline said into the continuing silence. "He's done it again." Several people snickered.

Face flushed, Rick dug turquoise pants with black stripes down the sides and white hats with turquoise bills from the box. Women! he thought to himself in exasperation. He'd never understand them.

"I think they're kind of pretty," Betty said in a loud voice. Half a dozen heads swiveled in her direction. Betty's cheeks turned a fiery red at the sudden attention and she stared down at the tablecloth, bravado evaporated.

Within a minute of her comment, most of the team had gone to the front to inspect the garments up close. Marty stayed in her seat. Poor Rick! Those broad bands of color were like nothing she'd ever seen before on women's uniform shirts.

"You know," Pauline was heard to comment, "those stripes are going to make Vicky look like the Queen Mary."

Vicky held up a shirt and pushed out her chest. "Yeah," she drawled in a pleased tone, "they sure will."

Rick took advantage of the confusion to walk swiftly over to where Marty was still seated. After greeting the others, he stared down at her, causing her pulse first to hesitate and then to surge forward in double time.

"I want to talk to you," he said, face unsmiling.

Renewed hope bubbled through Marty's veins like expensive champagne, to be quickly subdued

182

by the gravity of his expression. Before she could answer, Pat was calling for everyone to be seated so they could continue.

"Later," Rick said tersely, and turned away.

After presenting him with the sponsor's trophy from Nationals and giving Vera an autographed team picture in appreciation for backing them during the regular season, Pat began presenting individual gag awards.

Vicky got a large set of false eyelashes cut from felt, sprayed gold and glued to a small piece of plywood. Her award was for most eyelashes lost in the outfield during a single season. Louise received a small mitt with a large safety pin attached, also sprayed gold and mounted on a stand that looked suspiciously like an empty toilet paper roll. She had set a record for forgetting her mitt either at home or in the dugout.

Pat finished with several more awards that poked fun at other players, then proceeded to pass out bronze plaques provided by Rick. Each was engraved with the player's name, the year, and the team name.

Pat accomplished each presentation with a few facts about the woman's accomplishments. When she got to Marty, the list of statistics was impressive. Cheeks flushed with nervousness, Marty indicated that she wanted to say a few words. When the applause died down, she spoke into the mike.

"I'll keep this short, so we can get on to the dancing and drinking," she said, looking at each of her teammates in turn.

"Softball's been good to me, and I've been real lucky to play with a great bunch like you for the last few years." Her voice wavered and she swallowed hard before continuing.

183

"I always felt a need to prove myself," she continued slowly. "To compete, to be the best." She stopped and looked directly at her father. "I've come to realize that I don't have anything to prove after all. The acceptance I went after was there all along."

Seeing her father pull a handkerchief from his pocket, Marty felt her own eyes mist over. She turned her gaze to Rick, who was sitting bolt upright, dark eyebrows pulled together into a puzzled frown.

"The game has given me a lot," she continued. "And I've given my best back. Now it's time to get on with my life."

A buzz of voices rose around her.

She smiled at them all. "That's right," she said. "I'm officially announcing my retirement."

The room was filled with groans, shrieks of surprise, and questions. Marty waited for everyone to quiet down before continuing.

Pat touched her shoulder. "Are you sure?" she asked. "We hate to lose you."

"It's right for me," Marty answered. "I know now that it's time."

In all the confusion, she didn't notice Rick approach the podium. Before she could ask what he was doing, he picked her up and threw her over his shoulder, strong fingers burning through the thin fabric of her blouse before one hand splayed across her bottom to hold her steady. As he leaned toward the mike, his deep voice cut across the laughter of the crowd and Marty's loud protests.

"Marty and I are leaving now," he said coolly. "The rest of you stay and enjoy the dancing. Have a good time."

Lifting her head, the last thing Marty saw before

184

the door swung shut behind them was the broad smile on her father's face. Embarrassed, she protested Rick's cavalier treatment of her all the way down the front walk of the hired hall.

Ignoring her steady barrage of questions, he stuffed her inelegantly into the Mercedes and climbed in behind the wheel. "Fasten your seat belt" was all he said as he pulled away from the curb. The car turned in the direction of his house. Suddenly excited, Marty mutely obeyed.

Rick was driving with controlled madness and she didn't want to distract him. She kept quiet until they reached his house. The car squealed to a stop in the circular driveway. Jerking open her door, he hauled Marty into his arms. She was grateful he didn't throw her over his shoulder again. Taking the front steps the way Sherman took Atlanta, pausing only long enough to fumble open the front door and kick it shut, he set Marty down and pulled her into an embrace that threatened to crack her ribs.

His kiss contained neither tender tribute nor gentle coaxing. Instead it was a fervent assault that fed a rampant hunger growing for weeks. Marty returned every bit of his fire with a passion she made no attempt to disguise.

Tears formed before her eyelids, which were squeezed shut, as she absorbed his scent, his touch, and the warmth of his body beneath her caressing hands. Releasing her mouth, he dropped kisses on her nose, cheeks, and eyelashes. Then his lips glided to the curve of one small ear.

"I missed you like hell," he breathed. "I was going to tell you that I wanted you back on any terms. Then you made that announcement and I couldn't wait."

185

Marty smiled up at him. "They'll be talking about our grand exit for weeks," she said.

"Let them. I've got you right where I want you." His eyes darkened with passion as he asked a silent question.

"Not quite where I want to be," Marty said softly.

"I know we have a lot to talk about," Rick murmured as one finger traced the bow of her mouth. "Could it wait till later?"

Marty laughed at his pleading tone. "Later," she agreed as he led the way down the hall. Everything had happened so quickly that she needed to feel his warm flesh against hers before she could really believe that they were together again. Their fingers were entwined as if Rick was also reluctant to lose touch for even a moment.

They removed each other's clothing with many pauses for quick kisses and tender caresses. Happiness swelled Marty's heart within her chest each time that Rick's loving gaze met her own. Drumming pulses thundered in her ears when his mouth touched her skin. Nerve endings she had tried to ignore for days quivered to life under the heated touch of his fingers. The groan that rumbled from deep in his chest when Marty's hands smoothed over the broad expanse was music to her ears. She gasped from between parted lips as Rick's head lowered and his tongue touched the puckered tips of her breasts. Her arms encircled him, fingers buried in his hair, as they sank onto the wide bed.

"My God, how I love you," Rick growled before his mouth covered hers in a kiss that bore traces of desperation mixed with total possession.

It was much later that he propped himself up on

186

one elbow and brushed her mussed hair back from her forehead. "I love you," he said again, gazing into her eyes in the dim glow of a small lamp. They'd both murmured the words many times as they held and touched each other, needing to say and to hear the words that would reaffirm their devotion.

Rick leaned across Marty, pausing to place a kiss on her collarbone before sliding open the nightstand drawer. He withdrew a velvet box. Sitting up, he pulled Marty to him. "Will you marry me and join our lives together?" he asked, love blazing from his blue eyes.

Marty returned his ardent gaze, her lips trembling with joy. "Yes," she answered softly, "I will."

As she thanked the heavens for their second chance, and gazed lovingly at Rick's dark head over the small box, he snapped it open. Inside was a heart-shaped diamond solitaire.

"If you don't care for this ring, we can pick out something else together," he said, taking her left hand.

He slipped it onto her finger. It was too big and would have fallen off if he had let go. Marty chuckled, then curled her fingers to hold it in place. "I don't know if I can part with it long enough to have it sized," she commented. "I love it! When did you buy it?"

"Three days ago," Rick confessed.

Her eyebrows rose in puzzlement.

"It gave me hope," he continued. "It's hard to explain, but when I decided that there had to be a way for us to work things out, I bought the ring. It was a symbol to me that we would end up together. Do you think I'm crazy?"

Marty wrapped her arms around his neck. "I

187

think you're sweet," she murmured, nibbling at his ear. "And I love you very much."

"You don't have to give up playing," he said. "We could arrange our schedules somehow. I was bullheaded and jumped to conclusions before."

Marty placed two fingers over his mouth. "Shh," she instructed. "You weren't either. I was being selfish and unrealistic. Not to mention stubborn."

He nodded, straight-faced. "Well, I guess I see your point. You *were* being stubborn." The dimple that always fascinated her appeared briefly in his tanned cheek just before she hit him with a pillow, laughing.

"I was only trying to be agreeable," he protested, throwing up an arm to defend himself from another blow.

"Don't be too agreeable," Marty cautioned him, "or I may have to strike you out again, just to keep you in your place."

"Don't count on that," Rick answered. "I'm a pretty fast learner. A couple more pitches and I would have cranked one over the trees."

"Ha!"

"Want me to prove it?"

"Anytime, sport, anyplace!"

The room grew silent as Rick's attention strayed and he began to caress the soft curve of Marty's breast. "Yeah, a rematch might be a good idea," he murmured. His mouth covered hers and his hand searched for the switch on the bedside lamp. "Later, much, much later. Right now we have better things to do."

Now you can reserve August's
Candlelights
before they're published!

- ♥ You'll have copies set aside for _you_ the instant they come off press.
- ♥ You'll save yourself precious shopping time by arranging for _home delivery._
- ♥ You'll feel proud and efficient about organizing a system that _guarantees_ delivery.
- ♥ You'll avoid the disappointment of not finding _every_ title you want and need.

ECSTASY SUPREMES $2.75 each

- ☐ **133 SUSPICION AND DESIRE,** JoAnna Brandon . 18463-0-11
- ☐ **134 UNDER THE SIGN OF SCORPIO,** Pat West . . 19158-0-27
- ☐ **135 SURRENDER TO A STRANGER,** Dallas Hamlin 18421-5-12
- ☐ **136 TENDER BETRAYER,** Terri Herrington 18557-2-18

ECSTASY ROMANCES $2.25 each

- ☐ **450 SWEET REVENGE,** Tate McKenna 18431-2-10
- ☐ **451 FLIGHT OF FANCY,** Jane Atkin 12649-5-11
- ☐ **452 THE MAVERICK AND THE LADY,**
  Heather Graham 15207-0-34
- ☐ **453 NO GREATER LOVE,** Jan Stuart 16377-3-28
- ☐ **454 THE PERFECT MATCH,** Anna Hudson 16947-X-37
- ☐ **455 STOLEN PASSION,** Alexis Hill Jordan 18394-4-23

- ☐ **1** _THE TAWNY GOLD MAN,_ Amii Lorin 18978-0-35
- ☐ **2** _GENTLE PIRATE,_ Jayne Castle 12981-8-33

At your local bookstore or use this handy coupon for ordering:

DELL READERS SERVICE—DEPT. B1143A
P.O. BOX 1000, PINE BROOK, N.J. 07058

Please send me the above title(s). I am enclosing $ _____ (please add 75c per copy to cover postage and handling). Send check or money order no cash or CODs Please allow 3-4 weeks for shipment. CANADIAN ORDERS please submit in U.S. dollars

Ms Mrs Mr _____

Address_____

City State_____ Zip _____

JAYNE CASTLE

excites and delights you with tales of adventure and romance

_____**TRADING SECRETS**

Sabrina had wanted only a casual vacation fling with the rugged Matt. But the extraordinary pull between them made that impossible. So did her growing relationship with his son—and her daring attempt to save the boy's life.
19053-3-15 $3.50

_____**DOUBLE DEALING**

Jayne Castle sweeps you into the corporate world of multimillion dollar real estate schemes and the very private world of executive lovers. Mixing business with pleasure, they made _passion_ their bottom line.
12121-3-18 $3.95